"This book made my face hurt! Relentlessly fu[illegible]
Rob Biddulph, author of *Peanut Jo[illegible]*

"Ted and Nancy are my favorite [illegible]es EVER."
[illegible]chon, [illegible] *Tom Gates*

"You're in for a treat!"
Selom Sunu, illustrator of *Look Both Ways*

"PURE GENIUS!"
Louie Stowell, author of *Otherland*

"Made us laugh out loud."
Jim Smith, author of *Barry Loser*

"FANTASTIC."
LAUREN LAVERNE

"FIZZES WITH MAD ENERGY. BRILLIANTLY ADDICTIVE."
PHIL EARLE, AUTHOR OF *WHEN THE SKY FALLS*

"UTTERLY HILARIOUS."
SOPHY HENN, AUTHOR OF *PIZAZZ*

"Like *Watership Down*, but funny. You'll laugh hysterically on every page."
Caitlin Moran

"I want to be friends with Ted and Willow!"
Eliza, age 7

Oh gosh, that is HIGH PRAISE indeed.

For Noah.

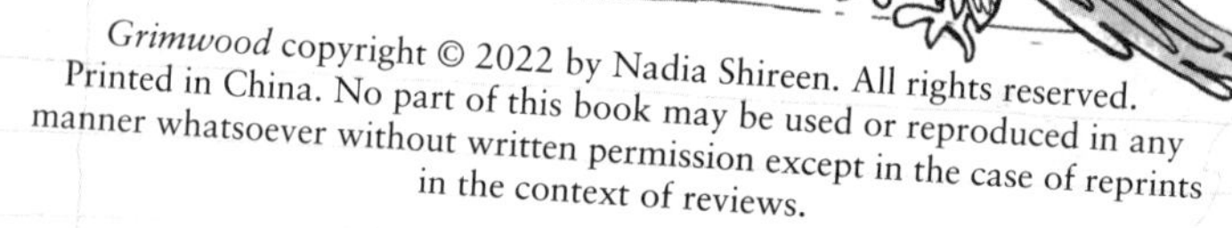

Andrews McMeel Publishing
a division of Andrews McMeel Universal
1130 Walnut Street, Kansas City, Missouri 64106

www.andrewsmcmeel.com

Grimwood was first published in Great Britain in 2021
by Simon & Schuster UK Ltd.

Simon & Schuster UK Ltd
1st Floor, 222 Gray's Inn Road, London
WC1X 8HB

www.simonandschuster.co.uk

23 24 25 26 27 SDB 10 9 8 7 6 5 4 3 2 1

Paperback ISBN: 978-1-5248-8225-9
Hardcover ISBN: 978-1-5248-8226-6

Library of Congress Control Number: 2022949704

Made by:
RR Donnelley (Guangdong) Printing Solutions Company Ltd
Address and location of manufacturer:
No. 2, Minzhu Road, Daning, Humen Town,
Dongguan City, Guangdong Province, China 523930
1st Printing – 1/2/23

NO REAL ANIMALS WERE HARMED
IN THE MAKING OF THIS BOOK

NADIA SHIREEN

Grimwood
Warning: Map completely useless
THE BIG CITY
BUNNYVILLE
TITUS'S CAMPER

THE MAGIC TOWER
The small pond
smelly puddle, nobody knows why
Abandoned old fox den
tiny hotel only for ants

I'm **ERIC DYNAMITE** and I'll be popping up every now and then with my thoughts. Bet you weren't expecting that, were you? It's a surprise to me too, to be honest. I'm normally a bus driver.

woodlouse
(a fancy name for a roly-poly)

Anyway . . . turn the page for some mind-bending storytime excitement!

ILLUS. 102. THE VERTICAL LEAF ARRANGEMENT OF THE GREY POPLAR

CHAPTER ONE

Ted and Nancy

This is Ted.

And this is Nancy.

Like a lot of foxes, they lived in a big city. Nancy was the bravest and boldest fox Ted had ever known. He couldn't remember having a mom or a dad, but he had always had Nancy. She made sure he had food and somewhere warm to sleep.

Apart from looking after Ted, Nancy liked to wander around the city with her friends. She knew every street, every dark alley, every dumpster, and every hiding place. Nancy was TOUGH. She had no time for laughing or sniffing flowers or reading comics. But Nancy didn't need those things, oh no.

Ted, on the other hand, was a sweet little fox cub. He liked staying close to the den, which was hidden inside some spiky holly bushes in the corner of a huge park. Ted liked to roll around on the grass in the sunshine, snuffle through twigs and leaves, and lick up dropped ice-cream cones. Every now and then Nancy would trot by and drop off a snack for him.

Nancy preferred coffee.

It kept her ALERT.

Fig. 1

Fig. 2.

Though sometimes, if she drank too much, she would shake and bark and Ted would have to sit on her head to calm her down.

Yes, Ted and Nancy were a great pair of foxes, and they had everything they needed. Well, almost everything. Lately, Ted had noticed a weird, achy feeling in his chest. He had it whenever he watched Nancy trot away, leaving him alone in the den. He had it when he saw her chatting with her fox friends, Bin and Hedge. He had it when he saw the cute little humans in the park holding hands with their big humans. Sometimes he would have it at night, when he would sit on top of a large rock, look up at the big, dark sky, and give a heavy sigh.

One afternoon, Ted was curled up in the den when he heard music. Someone was playing the guitar. And then a high, reedy little voice began to sing a gentle song.

Oh, hello, my great big pal
Oh, hello, my sweet amigo
I never feel alone
When my best friend comes to town

Won't you hold my hand and smile
And together you and me
Will laugh and sing and dance and skip
And never be lonelyyyy . . .

Ted scrambled out of the den.

"That's it!" he cried. "I'm **LONELY!** I need friends."

He looked at the grasshopper who had sung the song.

"Hello! Will **YOU** be my friend, little grasshopper?" he asked. "*You* like to sing, *I* like to sing—we have a lot in common!"

"Get lost," said the grasshopper, boinging away.

Ted's tail drooped, but then he rubbed his paws together. At least now that he knew what the achy feeling in his heart was, he could try to fix it. And there was no time like the present.

Just then, he heard a noise coming from the dumpster.

"Coo... Coo... Coo ... Is there any ketchup in there?"

"Coo... Coo... Can't see any. Ooh, what about mayo?"

"That'll have to do, I suppose. . . Coo. . . Coo. . . "

Two pigeons were perched on the edge of the dumpster, pecking out crumbs of chips and apple and goodness knows what.

"Hello!" said Ted. He'd seen these pigeons before. One of them only had one foot, and the other was wearing sunglasses.

"Go away," said the one-footed pigeon.

"My name's Ted. I recognize you!" said Ted.

The pigeon glared at him.

"I bet you do," said the pigeon wearing sunglasses. "Your sister bit his foot off."

Ted blushed. "Oh . . ." he said. "I'm so sorry."

"What do you want, kid?" said the one-footed pigeon.

"Well," said Ted shyly. "It's just that I've seen you guys around and I get a bit lonely all on my own in the den. I was wondering, um . . . would you like to be my friends?"

The pigeons shook their heads.

"You must be joking, pal," said the one-footed pigeon. "I'd like to keep my other foot, thank you."

And they hopped and fluttered off to another dumpster far, far away.

"Oh well," said Ted, patting himself on the head. "At least you tried. That's the main thing."

He was about to make up a song about it when he spotted two shadowy figures perched on a park bench. They had whiskers! They had tails! Ted's nose twitched in fear. **CATS!** One of them was draining a can of something into its mouth, while the other one was licking itself somewhere rude. Both of them stopped every now and then to do some evil yowling.

Ted whimpered and tried to creep away. He lifted one paw and put it down gently . . . and lifted another paw and put it down gently . . . and lifted *another* paw and—

"AWOOOGA! Let's party!"

Ted had accidentally stepped on Sharon the Party Crow.

"SHHHHHHH!" shhhh'd Ted.

"Party time—ACTIVATED!"

said Sharon, who then blew a kazoo extremely loudly.

The cats jolted upright and glared at Ted with scary yellow eyes.

"Hissss," they hissed.

"AAAARGH!" aaaargh'd Ted.

He ran back to the den as quick as his furry little legs could carry him.

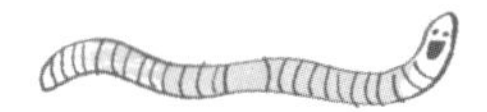

Nancy was in the den with her pals, Bin and Hedge. They were making silly faces and taking photos of each other on their phones.

Ted dove into the den, wide-eyed and panting.

"What's up with you?" said Nancy.

He pointed behind him, whimpering and jumping in place.

Nancy grabbed Ted's ears and slowly stroked them until he calmed down.

"C-c-c-cats!" he eventually gasped.

"Was it HER?" asked Nancy sharply.

Ted shook his head.

"Well, don't freak out then! The other cats ain't gonna do nothin' to you, Ted."

Ted sighed and shuffled over to his corner of the den.

Nancy rolled her eyes at Bin and Hedge. She and Ted were going to have to have a talk.

"See you later, OK?" she said.

"All right, Nance, later," said Bin.

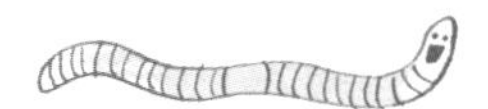

Nancy sat next to Ted, who was curled up in a corner cuddling Slipper, which was an old slipper with a smiley face drawn on it. He'd had it since he was a tiny cub.

"When are Mom and Dad coming home, Nancy?" Ted said.

Nancy sighed.

"I dunno, Ted," she replied. "They never said."

"But . . . they are coming back, aren't they? I'd love to know what they look like."

Nancy didn't answer. She just gazed into space while Ted sat quietly, listening to the patter of the rain and the distant thrum of traffic.

After a while, he spoke again.

"Nance, why do the cats hate us so much?"

Nancy curled her bushy tail around Ted.

"They don't *all* hate us," she said. "Just some of them. And you *know* why that is, don't you?"

"Is it because of that really horrible cat?" said Ted.

"Yeah," said Nancy. "It's because of that really horrible cat."

CHAPTER TWO
That really horrible cat

This is Princess Buttons.

She is a cat. A really horrible cat.

The story goes that a few years ago, Princess Buttons lived in a huge mansion. Her owner was a rich old lady who wore very fancy clothes, even if she was just going to the corner store to buy some of the fancy cat food her pampered pet liked. Princess Buttons went everywhere with her, carried around in a large purple handbag so that she never got her precious paws dirty. Her life was perfect.

But then one day, the old lady choked on a pickle and was taken away in an ambulance. Princess Buttons lay on the satin sheets of the old lady's bed and yowled. Many days passed, and eventually she knew in her bones that the old lady was never coming back. Princess Buttons would have to make her own way in the big, bad world.

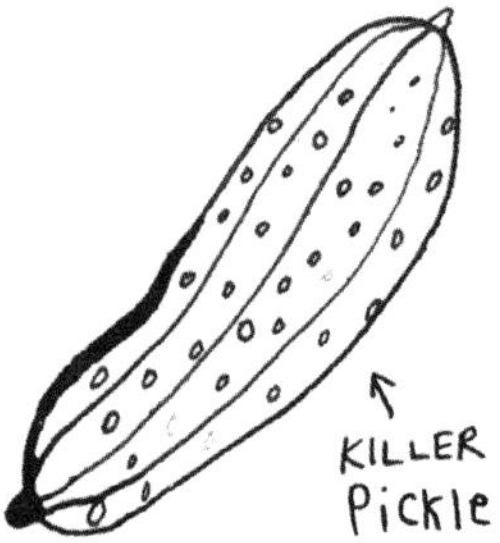

She roamed the streets, hungry and lost.

But then one day she sniffed a waft of something fabulous. **"Gnnnnnnnnf!"** said Princess Buttons, and she licked her lips. She trotted toward the smell, expecting to see a grand department store, or maybe a fancy restaurant. But instead she found . . .

Well. It certainly wasn't fancy, but to Princess Buttons it looked like heaven. She darted down the alley next to the shop, her tummy rumbling. She scaled the brick wall, tumbled over the top, and saw . . .

Foxes. So many foxes.

They were tearing apart the Speedy Chicken trashbags that had been piled high throughout the day, stealing all the greasy, gooey food inside. Princess Buttons could just about make out three massive dumpsters, each the size of a small car. Cats, rats, pigeons, and mice were hopping around too, chewing on bits of gristle and half-eaten pita bread.

Princess Buttons skulked along the ground and pounced on some leftover fried chicken. Oh, it was delicious! She'd never tasted anything like it, and she gnawed the bones clean in seconds.

"Ooh, may I?" said another cat, pointing at the leftover bones.

"What?" snapped Princess Buttons.

"Don't you want the bones?" asked the cat gently.

"No," said Princess Buttons, who was used to eating soft, delicate morsels of meat.

"Great!" said the other cat, who began to suck and chew on the chicken bones.

"You must be new around here," he said cheerfully, after a while. "I'm Bingo! Nice to meet you. Word of advice—you don't wanna let anything go to waste. There's just about enough food to go around. But only just. There's a system, you see."

And he returned to his bone-crunching.

Princess Buttons frowned.

"What do you mean . . . 'a system'?" she asked.

"Well," said Bingo, licking his lips. "It's simple really. There are three dumpsters.

The foxes eat out of the blue one, the cats have the green one, and the rats, pigeons, mice, and everyone else have the red one."

Princess Buttons wrinkled her nose.

"You...you mean you *share*?" she said, barely managing to get the word out.

"MMmm-hmm!" nodded Bingo.

Princess Buttons felt her hackles rising. SHARE? She had never had to share a thing in her life. She growled and wrinkled her nose. It all sounded VERY WRONG. Something would have to be done.

Over the next few weeks, Princess Buttons devoured as much food from Speedy Chicken as she could get her paws on. Night after night, she sat by the green dumpster, waiting for the bags of leftovers to arrive, and **HISSED** at anyone who dared to get too close. She got greasier and grimier. Very soon, everyone in the Big City knew who she was.

"Why are you all so soft?" she said to the other cats one evening. "You let those filthy FOXES take all the best pieces.

Some of the cats murmured in agreement, though many just carried on licking their bottoms.

"We cats need to stand up for ourselves!" hooted Princess Buttons, who was by now gathering a small crowd. "For too long we've had to sit by and watch the foxes eat up every last bit of food around here . . ."

Bingo stopped licking his bottom and raised his paw to remind everyone about the dumpster-sharing system, but nobody seemed interested in listening to him.

"It's time to take back control of our dumpsters!" yelled Princess Buttons, raising a clenched paw in the air.

Most of the cats rolled their eyes and sauntered away. But some of them cheered.

"Take back our dumpsters!" they shouted. "Kick out the foxes!"

Princess Buttons waited until the group of cats fell silent. She stared at them with her beady little eyes, then bellowed, "We will not rest until all the dumpsters are ours!"

The cats cheered even louder. Some of them even started banging tin cans together.

"Let battle commence," snarled Princess Buttons, and angrily bit the end off a sausage.

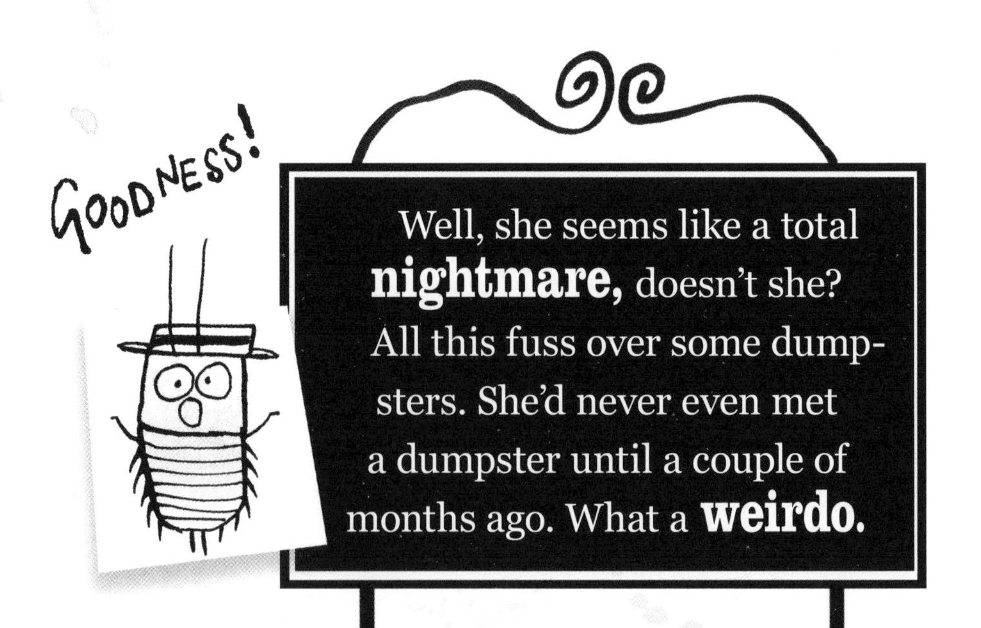

CHAPTER THREE
The hot dog bun of doom

Miserable old Princess Buttons couldn't stand any of the foxes, but the fox she hated the most was Nancy—because Nancy was brave, and clever, and not at all scared of her. Princess Buttons tried scheme after wicked scheme to get rid of the foxes. But even if she spooked Ted from time to time, she couldn't outsmart Nancy. And it was driving her bananas.

"She's something else, that cat," said Nancy. She and Ted had just arrived back at the den after a run-in with Princess Buttons at the dumpsters, where she had pelted them with rotten bananas. "Shoulda stayed in her fancy house instead of coming down here and trying to cause trouble."

"She won't hurt us, will she, Nance?" asked Ted, peeling a bit of banana skin off his fur.

"Not while I'm around," said Nancy. "Just don't go down to the dumpsters by yourself, OK?"

Ted was a good little ~~banana~~ fox and he tried very hard to do what Nancy told him. But the ache in his chest hadn't gone away. He felt it most strongly when Nancy was out chasing cars with Bin and Hedge while he sat all alone, staring at the stars. And that's how Ted found himself one fateful night. He was bored, lonely... and so hungry. He really wanted a hot dog. He closed his eyes, but even then all he could see were dancing hot dogs singing, "Eat me!" He moaned and patted his stomach. Even a good little fox like Ted couldn't ignore a grumbling tummy.

Ted crept out of the den and made his way to Speedy Chicken, keeping his eyes open for Princess Buttons and her gang of horrible cats. His heart was beating wildly as he scrambled over the wall. He checked that the coast was clear, then scampered over to the edge of the fox dumpster, where he sat and watched a group of rodents exercising. The one-footed pigeon was pecking away at a tray of salad, while his friend was trying to complete a newspaper crossword. It seemed to Ted that everyone he saw had a friend, except him. Princess Buttons, meanwhile, was nowhere to be seen.

Ted turned his attention to the dumpster. One bag had already been torn open, and there, lying on top of a pile of banana peels (*ewwww*, thought Ted), was a great big, fat, juicy hot dog. *Mmmmmm*, thought Ted. It looked almost as good as the hot dogs of his dreams. A delicious smoky sausage, dripping with ketchup and mustard, nestled inside a white, soft, fluffy bun.

He picked it up, shut his eyes, and chomped.

"YEEEEEOOOOOOWWWW!"

"Mmmfffgnnaaargh!"

yelled Ted.

He looked down, and in his paws saw a thick, stubby cat tail stuffed inside the hot dog bun.

Ted panicked. He clutched the hot dog (and the tail) to his chest and leapt from the dumpster.

Princess Buttons had slunk out from under a pile of garbage and was yowling in agony. The other cats began to circle her.

"Now you're in trouble, you little squirt!" one of them hissed at Ted, baring its teeth.

Ted's heart was thumping and he felt like he might cry.

"Oh yeah? Says who?" growled a voice from the shadows.

"Nancy!" yelped Ted.

Nancy, Bin, and Hedge formed a circle around Ted.

"It was an accident!" Ted whimpered. "I didn't know she was there!"

Princess Buttons had staggered to her feet.

"That's it," she growled, and pointed at Ted. "You're dead, little foxy."

Everything happened very quickly after that.

Nancy glanced at Bin and Hedge, who both gave her a nod. Then she grabbed Ted by the scruff of the neck and leapt over the Speedy Chicken wall.

"RUN,"

said Nancy, putting him down.

They ran and ran and ran until they were back at the den.

"I think we're going to have to find

somewhere else to live for a while," said Nancy, panting heavily.

"No!" cried Ted.

Nancy kicked a can in frustration. It bounced off a trash can and hit an unsuspecting snail in the face.

"We can't leave! I thought we were going to wait for Mom and Dad to come back!" cried Ted. "You said that one day they would come back!"

Nancy looked at her scruffy baby brother. He had big, trusting brown eyes and a little tuft of hair that stuck up between his ears. When he looked sad it made her heart hurt. She sighed.

"Listen. I promised them I'd always keep you

safe. But I don't know if we're going to be safe here anymore. I mean, you just bit Princess Buttons's tail off, Ted!"

"I didn't mean to," Ted sniffled. He picked up the scraggly thing and waved it around.

"What should I do with it, Nance?"

"Just shove it in your bag," she snapped. Nancy rubbed her head. "Buttons is gonna be furious—we need to lie low. Pack up your stuff. Soon enough she'll have told all the cats in the Big City, and we'll have nowhere to hide."

"B-b-but where will we go?" whimpered Ted.

"I dunno yet. I'm thinking. Look, you can leave Mom and Dad a note just in case, OK?"

Dear Mom and Dad

Hello! I hope you're both Ok. If you're reading this then you've finally come back to the park. Hooray! Except also boo, because me and Nance have to leave for a bit. This horrible cat has been bullying us forever. Now I accidentally bit off her tail and she's really not happy about it. I don't know where we're going but if you find this note PLEASE don't forget us. I will try and send more letters. I am a lot bigger now than when you last saw me, probably. Nancy takes care of me really well so don't worry.

I love you

TED xxxxx

Ted was struggling to walk under the weight of his backpack. Nancy was frowning and chewing her lip as they trudged on. *She can't be worried,* thought Ted. *Nancy is never worried.*

Then something bonked Ted on the head.

"Ow!"

It was an empty soda can.

"Many apologies!" came a voice from behind him. "Over here!"

Ted rubbed his head and looked behind him. He saw a furry little brown thing huffing and puffing toward him. As it got closer he could see it was a rat. And as it got even closer, he could see it was a rat wearing a T-shirt with a smiley face on it.

"Hello!" said the rat, holding out a friendly paw. "I'm Sven! So good to meet you!"

"Um . . . hello," said Ted, waving at the chubby rodent panting at his feet. "Don't I know you?"

"Yes, I am always at the Speedy Chicken dumpsters doing my exercises!" said the rat. "I am a super-duper fitness rat. Behold!"

The rat suddenly dropped to the ground and did three really fast push-ups. Then he did a couple that were a little slower. And then he did one that took absolutely forever, but Ted pretended not to notice.

When Sven finally finished his push-up, he turned to Ted. "Listen up, foxy, you've always seemed like a nice kid," he said.

"TED!" barked Nancy. She had stopped under a streetlight and was glaring down the sidewalk at him. "HURRY UP."

"I saw what happened at the dumpsters earlier. I know you guys need to hide out somewhere for a while," said Sven. "So here. Take this."

The little rat pushed a bit of crumpled-up paper into Ted's paws.

"What is it?" asked Ted.

"A map," said Sven. "It'll take you somewhere safe, far away from here. A beautiful, magical forest."

Ted's ears pricked up.

"A forest? A real-life forest? With leaves and grass and mud and stuff?"

Sven smiled. "Sure, yes, a forest! Full of animals being wild and free, and no nasty cats or dumpsters or any of that stuff. Exactly the kind of place a fox should be."

Ted hopped from foot to foot. This sounded brilliant. He'd always wanted to live like a proper fox, running and digging about in the wild, getting muddy paws and freaking out bunnies.

Ted looked at the map.

"Grimwood?" he said, looking down at Sven.

"Yep," said Sven. He had a faraway, misty look in his eyes. "Grimwood. My home."

"Why did you move to the Big City?" asked Ted.

Sven looked dreamily into the distance.

"For love," he said mysteriously. Then he shut his eyes and screamed, "BELINDA! WHY????"

into the air, before dabbing at his eyes with a tiny handkerchief.

"Sorry about that," said Sven, collecting himself. "Anyway, yes, Grimwood! You must go."

"And you're sure we won't get eaten?" said Ted.

"Um . . . no! I mean yes. I mean no. OK, maybe," said Sven. "First, you must find a rat called Binky Snuffhausen. He knows who I am. Tell him who you are, and then you will be safe! Well, probably."

"Wow!" said Ted. "Thanks, Sven."

And he bent down to shake the little rat's paw. But Sven had already strapped on his rollerblades and was zooming away, back toward Speedy Chicken.

"No worries, kid!" he called back. "Good luck. And, remember—whatever you do, find BINKY SNUFFHAUSEN! That's BINKY SNUFFHAUSEN!!!"

CHAPTER FOUR

The death of Binky Snuffhausen

"Oh, what a beautiful morning!" said Binky Snuffhausen, throwing open the curtains and beaming at the world outside his window. He felt like the happiest rat. He'd had a delicious breakfast of pancakes topped with whipped cream, sliced bananas, and a large drizzle of maple syrup. Yesterday, his girlfriend, Sonia, had told him that she loved him. And he'd finally finished his thousand-piece jigsaw puzzle of the Eiffel Tower, which had taken forever. Binky checked out his reflection in the mirror.

"Looking good, Binkster!" he said, giving himself the thumbs-up. He was having a *really* good hair day, which is often difficult for a rat.

There was a FLUP sound by his front door, and Binky noticed that a letter had flopped onto his doormat. "How exciting!" he squealed, because it was always fun to get mail. "Letter, letter, letter!" he trilled, trotting over to the doormat.

"Letter, letter, letter," he whispered, tearing open the envelope.

He unfolded the paper inside and gasped.

CONGRATULATIONS!

Dear Mr Bonky Sniffhausen,

You have won $3,500,000 for absolutely no reason at all! Simply take this letter to Grimwood Bank and present it to the manager who will give you bundles of cash immediately. Go on, then. Right now, OK? Thanks, byeeee!

Yours sincerely,

The Grimwood Bank Manager

Binky clutched the letter to his chest. It really was the best day of his life!

He put on his best hat and boots, stuffed the letter into his waistcoat pocket, and opened the door of his cardboard box. He stepped out into the glorious sunshine and took a big, deep breath of fresh air.

"How I love living in wonderful Grimwood!" he said. "It's just a perfect day! Nothing, absolutely nothing, could go wrong on a day as beautiful as this."

And he was just about to start whistling a cheerful song when his head was bitten off by a massive eagle.

CHAPTER FIVE
The weird giant horse thing

Pamela (who was the massive eagle) flew back to her nest and dabbed at her beak with a handkerchief. "Oh, Binky," she said. "You were just as tasty as I hoped you'd be." She ruffled her feathers, did a delicate burp, and settled down at her typewriter to write another fake letter to deliver to tomorrow's victim.

A large owl silently swooped down next to her.

"That was very mean," said Frank, who had a noble owly face and eyebrows like giant caterpillars. "Binky was a nice guy."

"A bird has to eat." Pamela shrugged. "Anyway, I only took his head. He's still got his arms and legs, it's not all bad."

Frank was about to reply when he noticed something strange. Extremely strange. So strange that he actually said, "How strange!" out loud.

Something mysterious was moving around in the leaves below. He flew next to Pamela and silenced her typewriter with a firm claw.

"Look, Pamela." He nodded. "Down there. Something's moving."

A patch of grass beneath the oak tree was shifting, as if something huge was digging up to the surface from deep underground.

"It's the GIANT MOLE OF BRATISLAVA*!" said Pamela, who was prone to panic. "Or the worms! The worms have finally turned! I knew it would happen one day! They've come together from miles around to form a WORM ARMY!!!"

*Please note, as far as we know there is no such thing as the Giant Mole of Bratislava.

"Calm down, Pamela," said Frank, his eyes narrowing. He was getting ready to swoop.

Suddenly there was a volcano of soil and leaves.

"THE WOORRRRRRRMS!" screamed Pamela, unhelpfully.

Frank watched as two figures crawled out of the ground. He squinted but he couldn't identify the mysterious creatures.

"I'm going to fetch Titus," he said, and swooped up into the sky.

The foxes looked around as they got their breath back. They had been digging for ages and their paws were tired and sore.

"Is this it?" said Ted, wiping mud from his eyes.

Nancy removed a worm from her nose and looked around some more.

"Hmm," she said.

She looked at Sven's map and turned it around a few times.

"Well?" said Ted. "What do you think, sis? Did the map work? Are we in the right place?"

"Hmm," she said again.

She gave the map a sniff. It was annoying her. She ate the map.

"Nancy!" cried Ted.

"It was looking at me funny," said Nancy.

The foxes gazed at their new surroundings for a while. Ted took some deep breaths. The air was so different. He couldn't smell cars, or humans, or fried chicken restaurants. And the trees! They towered high above his curious little foxy head.

"The branches look like a giant spider's web dancing across the sky," he whispered, clutching his paws together. He felt like writing a poem about it, but before he could ask Nancy for a pen she'd bonked him on the head with her phone.

"I can't get a stupid signal!" she barked. "Nightmare! Do you have one?"

"I don't have a phone, Nance," said Ted, rubbing his head. "You said I'm not allowed one until I'm older."

"Oh yeah," she said. "Hey, bend down for a second."

She climbed onto Ted's back and held her phone as high as she could, waving it around trying to find a signal.

All of a sudden there was a

as something swooped down from the sky and grabbed Nancy's phone.

Ted dove behind a log.

"Hey!" shouted Nancy. "Come back, you thieving scoundrel!"

But Pamela the eagle (for she was the thieving scoundrel) zoomed merrily into the sky. She did an evil cackle and a loop-de-loop before disappearing into the trees.

Ted slowly peeked out from behind the log.

"Wh . . . what was that?" he whimpered.

"A massive bird!" growled Nancy. "And it took my phone! It's gonna regret it, the stupid beakface."

"I think we should start looking for Binky," said Ted.

"Who?"

"Binky Snuffhausen! The rat Sven told us about. He'll be able to tell us what to do."

Nancy scowled.

"We don't need anyone to tell us what to do,"

she snapped. “We’re in some worthless forest in the middle of nowhere. We just need to lie low for a while.”

“But what will we eat?” said Ted. “I can’t smell any chicken restaurants, or dumpsters, or food trucks.”

Nancy had to admit her brother had a point. All she’d ever known was the Big City. On the crowded and noisy streets, she knew how to handle herself. But now Nancy had an unfamiliar feeling in her tummy. It was a quiet, churning sensation, as if there were a washing machine in her belly.

“Want a gingersnap, Nance?” asked Ted gently. “I just found some at the bottom of my backpack.”

“Thanks, Ted,” said Nancy.

“What should I do with this?” asked Ted, unfurling Princess Buttons’s tail.

Nancy snorted. “Make a hat out of it for

all I care," she said, stretching and yawning.

The foxes lay down on a fallen tree trunk and munched thoughtfully on their cookies.

After a while Ted gave a contented sigh.

"It's peaceful here, isn't it, sis?" he said. The foxes were still dirty from the journey, but the midday heat was drying up the mud. Pleasing clumps of it crumbled off their fur onto the ground.

"It's too quiet if you ask me," said Nancy.

They had been traveling all night, and now that they were lying down, the foxes couldn't help but doze off into a deep, deep sleep.

Meanwhile, Frank the owl had flown halfway across Grimwood to find Titus, the mayor. Nobody could *quite* remember exactly why and how Titus had become mayor, but he was old and wise and everybody liked him.

Frank had to hammer his beak on the door of Titus's camper for a good ten minutes before he got an answer.

"WAKE UP, SIR!" he shouted.

"Frank! Sho shorry ..." mumbled Titus, opening the door. His eyes were half shut, and a bit of paper had stuck to his face with drool.

"Sorry to wake you, sir," said Frank. "But there's serious business afoot."

"Oh, I wasn't asleep, oh no! I was busy doing some . . . paperwork . . . things. Come in, come in."

"No time," said Frank. "Follow me. We've got *visitors*."

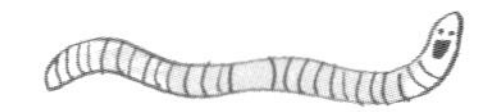

The first thing Ted saw when he opened his eyes was a massive pair of hairy nostrils.

"Arrgh!" he screamed.

Titus (for the nostrils belonged to him) staggered back.

"I'm sorry, little fellow, I didn't mean to startle you. Now . . . who's this on my head?"

On hearing Ted's scream, Nancy's eyes had opened instantly. Without thinking, she had flung herself onto Titus's antlers.

"Pick on someone your own size, you . . . you giant horse!" she yelled.

Titus stood up to his full height and shook his great big antlers from side to side until Nancy was flung through the air like a pancake.

“I’m so sorry,” said Titus, looking down at her. “It’s just, you were hurting my antlers.”

Nancy hopped back up on her feet and started shouting and snarling. Ted hid behind the log and closed his eyes.

"LEAVE US ALONE. HE'S JUST A KID! GET YOUR STUPID NOSE HOLES OUT OF OUR FACES," screamed Nancy.

Titus blinked.

“Hello there, young foxes! My name is Titus. Nice to meet you.”

And he stretched out a hoof in greeting.

“She’s definitely the feistier of the two,” said Frank, landing on Titus’s antler and nodding at Nancy.

“Hey!” shouted Nancy. “You stole my phone, bird!”

“That wasn’t me.” Frank shrugged.

Titus looked up at his old friend.

"Oh dear, has Pamela been at it again?" he sighed.

Frank gave a weary nod.

"She's a wild one, Titus. Her nest looks like a trash dump. It's an absolute nightmare."

Ted opened his eyes a little. He took a deep breath.

"My name's Ted!" he squeaked, peeking over the top of the log. "And she's Nancy!" He pointed a shaking paw toward his sister.

Titus regarded the foxes. They looked tired, hungry, and dirty. And he could smell that they were from the Big City. In fact—and it sounds a bit rude, but it was true—they absolutely *stank*. He could make out cars, buses, fried chicken, humans, dumpsters, and pizza boxes. *The poor little rascals must have been traveling for hours,* he thought to himself.

"Well, Ted and Nancy," he said, trying again with the whole shaking hooves thing. "Welcome to Grimwood! I'm the mayor, Titus Wildhorns."

"Oh, Nancy, we've made it! Grimwood! The map was right!" yelped Ted, forgetting to be scared and jumping up from behind the log. "We're looking for someone," he said to Titus.

"A rat, a rat called . . . Bonky Sniff . . . Snuff . . . something. Oh, what was it?"

Frank looked awkwardly at his feet.

"I don't suppose it was Binky Snuffhausen, was it?" he said.

"Yes!" said Ted, leaping into the air. "It WAS! Oh, hooray hooray! Please can we talk to Binky Snuffhausen?!"

Frank gave an embarrassed cough. He mumbled something very quietly.

"Eh? What was that, Frank?" said Titus, raising his big floppy ears.

Frank sighed.

"I said . . . I'm afraid Pamela bit Binky's head off this morning."

"No!" said Ted.

"Brutal," said Nancy, giving a low whistle.

"Oh, poor Binky!" cried Titus. "Is he all right?"

Frank blinked a couple of times.

"Um . . . *no*. He's dead."

"Oh NO!" said Titus. "Oh, Binky. He was such a cheerful fellow."

The stag bowed his head. Then there was a great big HONK as he blew his nose on a passing butterfly.

"We must give his body the burial it deserves. Where is the rest of poor little Binky Snuffhausen, Frank? Any idea?"

"Nope," said Frank quietly. "No idea."

Then he burped very loudly, and quickly covered his beak with his wing.

"What are we gonna do, Nance?" said Ted.

"They're gonna eat us up for sure!"

"Nobody's eating anybody, little fox," said Titus kindly (which made Frank do another sheepish cough).

Ted gulped. "A rat called Sven drew a map for us! I'd show it to you but . . . but Nancy ate it. Anyway, Sven said his friend Binky would make sure we were safe. But . . . but now Binky's dead and we've got nowhere else to go!"

Ted put his face in his paws and started to sob.

"Cheer up, Ted!" hissed Nancy, and then bared her teeth at Titus and Frank.

Titus looked at the scruffy pair. He could see that talking wasn't going to get them very far.

"Frank," he said, looking up at his friend and his large, powerful talons. "Let's go."

And before the foxes had a chance to protest, Frank spread his magnificent wings, hopped down from Titus's antlers, grabbed each fox by the scruff of the neck, and swooped into the air.

CHAPTER SIX
The den

"AaaaaaaAAAAAAAAAARRRRRGH!"

The foxes swung back and forth in Frank's talons as he swooped high over the tops of the tall, spiky trees. At one point they even flew through the clouds, which made their fur chilly and damp.

THUNK.

Frank dropped the foxes onto the ground.

"Sorry about that," said Titus, trotting casually out from the undergrowth. "It was the easiest way to get you here."

Nancy sniffed the air.

"Foxes," she murmured. "I can smell . . . other foxes. Where are they?"

"Ah," said Titus. "You are a smart one. Yes, apparently there used to be some foxes here in Grimwood. No idea where they are now, but their den is still here. You may as well have it before someone else starts using it as a vacation home."

"Pamela was thinking about storing her foot spa here," muttered Frank, examining his talons.

"Well, she'll have to find somewhere else," said Titus. "Ooh, I almost forgot—I swung by my place and brought you a few snacks!"

And he held out a wicker basket piled high with all sorts of tasty-looking things.

"Gosh!" said Ted, who was suddenly too hungry to be scared. "Thank you!"

He scampered over to the food. There were sandwiches, apples, carrots, grapes, and sticky buns. Nancy's tummy was rumbling so loudly everyone could hear it, but she didn't go near the basket. She was frowning at Titus and Frank.

"We can't give you anything for the food," she said.

"You don't need to give me anything," said Titus gently. He took a few steps back. "Come on, Frank. Let's leave them to get settled." Frank turned his beady gaze away from the foxes and swooped after Titus.

Nancy turned around to see Ted's bottom and tail hanging out of the basket. He'd dove in snout-first and was stuffing himself silly.

"Move," said Nancy, shoving him to one side and attacking the basket in a frenzy.

After about five seconds the foxes lay panting on the floor. They'd demolished every last scrap of food and it had been deeeelicious.

"Nance," said Ted, rubbing his furry belly. "I think those guys are just being nice to us, you know."

"Nobody's ever nice for no reason," said Nancy, licking crumbs of sandwich off her fur.

Ted thought for a while.

"But the big horse guy said we didn't need to give him anything."

“He’s just trying to placate us,” said Nancy. “That stupid bird stole my phone, remember? Also, he’s not a horse.”

“What is he, then?”

“I think he’s a moose.”

“I wonder who used to live here?” said Ted, plonking down his backpack and sniffing around.

Nancy took one of the blankets and hung it across the den, creating two separate spaces.

“You go here,” she barked. “And behind this curtain is MY space, got it? No little boy foxes allowed.”

Ted wrinkled his snout at her. As if he’d want to go in *Nancy’s* part of the den anyway. He preferred to keep things neat and tidy. He set to work dusting the floor, then unpacked the contents of his backpack. He still didn’t know what to do with Princess Buttons’s tail. It was an awkward reminder of the pickle they were in.

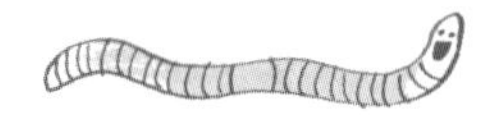

When Nancy woke up, she had absolutely no idea where she was. Then a gnat nibbled her armpit and she remembered she was in the countryside.

"Rise and shine, little foxes!" boomed a voice from outside the den. "Special delivery."

Nancy scrambled out to see Frank the owl swooping down to land. In his talons he was clutching two bottles filled with a strange, gloopy green liquid.

"Freshly made smoothies," he announced.

Nancy grabbed one of the bottles and gave it a sniff. Then she chugged the whole thing in seconds.

"You're welcome," said Frank.

Nancy wiped her snout with the back of her paw.

"Thanks," she grunted.

"It's not me you should be thanking, smiler," said Frank, stretching out his enormous wings.

Nancy grunted again and looked at the bottle.

"I don't know why he's bothering," snapped Frank. "His heart's too big for his own good, that stag. Where's the kid?"

Nancy rubbed her eyes and felt a sudden lurch of panic in her chest. Where *was* Ted?

"Ted!" she barked. "TED!"

She dashed back inside the den to double check but he wasn't there. She came back outside again and started to run around in circles, desperate to pick up his scent. Had Princess Buttons found them already? What if she'd kidnapped him?

"TED!" she cried.

"Morning, Nance!" said a bright voice from a nearby daisy patch.

"AAAAARGH!" yelled Nancy, leaping on top of him as if she needed to protect him from an explosion.

"Smoothie?" said Frank, raising an eyebrow at the bundle of fox by his feet.

"Oh, yes please!" said Ted, crawling out from under Nancy. He downed the drink in one gulp.

"Don't you DARE wander off from me, Ted!" panted Nancy.

"Oh . . . sorry, sis. I was just doing a little exploring."

Nancy growled.

"We're in HIDING, remember?"

"Aww, what an adorable little guy," said Frank, pecking at a bit of leftover breakfast worm from his talons. "There's plenty to see in Grimwood, young Ted."

Nancy was about to say something grumpy again when a mysterious object WHOOOOOSHED over their heads.

"TTRREEEEEBOOOOOOOONK!"

She threw herself on top of Ted again.

When she looked up, she saw a squirrel in a leotard splatted against a tree trunk.

Frank flew over and helped to peel it off.

"You're getting better at landing, Dolly," he said to the squirrel.

"Thanks, Frank!" squeaked Dolly, rubbing her head before scampering off.

Frank chuckled. "Always get a few splatterers at the beginning of treebonk season," he murmured.

"What?" said Nancy.

"Treebonk," said Frank, as if that explained everything.

"Ooooh!" said Ted, bouncing up and down. "How exciting!"

"Thanks for the drinks," said Nancy to Frank before he could say more about treebonk or anything else. "Now, if you'll excuse us, we've got some hiding to do."

And she gave her biggest HARRUMPH before dragging Ted back inside the den.

"Oh, Nance," moaned Ted. "I wanted to explore!"

"Since when are you so interested in exploring?" said Nancy.

"Since we arrived here!" said Ted. "It's safe, Nance, a million times safer than living in the Big City. Nothing bad ever happens in the countryside!"

Nancy pointed to Princess Buttons's tail, which she had pinned to the wall.

"THIS is why we're here, Ted. We're not on vacation. Now stay on your side of the den, and don't leave my sight, OK? I don't want your head getting bitten off like that Bonky Snuffington guy."

"Fine," snapped Ted. He shuffled over to his bed and cuddled Slipper. He hated being stuck inside when outside felt so fresh and exciting. He wanted to meet some new people and maybe, just maybe, make a *friend*. He lay on his bed and wrote a sad poem about loneliness, while Nancy practiced her martial arts moves.

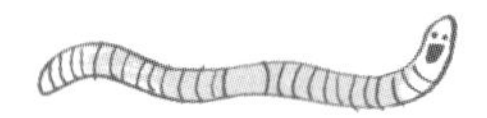

Hours passed. The light outside gradually changed as the day wore on. Nancy had exhausted herself and nodded off, just as Ted hoped she would. He stared at her, making sure she was absolutely, definitely fast asleep. When she gave a little snore, Ted took a deep breath and slowly crept out of the den . . .

The moment he poked his head outside, Ted took a big sniff. WOW! It really was mind-blowing. His nostrils were hit by so many weird and wonderful smells. Flowers! Leaves! Ants! Nettles! Bird poo!

He wandered around, running his paws through the long grass. The ground was a glorious carpet of wildflowers—dainty daisies, bright yellow buttercups, and long stalks of floppy hollyhocks. Ted scampered about and collected armfuls of them, pausing every now and then to shove his face into the petals and take a great big snort of happiness. He felt so happy, he decided to make up a song.

"HEY! Shut it!" shouted a very angry voice.

THUNK.

Someone threw an acorn at Ted's head.

Ted rubbed his nose and looked up.

In front of him was the teeniest, tiniest, cutest, and fluffiest bunny-wunny he had ever seen.

She threw another acorn at him.

"Ow!" said Ted.

"Some of us are trying to sleep!" squeaked the bunny. "Pipe down!"

"I'm so sorry," said Ted. "I was just—"

"I don't care!"

The flopperty-flipperty little bunny gave a shake of her soft, white fluffy tail, wrinkled her nose, and twitched her whiskers.

"Aw," said Ted. "You're such a cute little thing."

"WaaaaaAAAAAAAArrrrRGGGH!"

The bunny started thumping at Ted's head with her feet.

"I (**thwack**) . . . AM (**thwack**) . . . NOT (**thwack**) . . . *CUTE!* (**thwack thwack thwack**)."

"OK, OK!" pleaded Ted, shielding himself from the ferocious blows of the fluffy little nugget.

The bunny eventually stopped thwacking and looked at Ted thoughtfully.

"Your song was very good, actually," she said.

Ted clasped his paws together.

"Oh, thank you! I just made it up on the spot. I'm always doing that."

The bunny held out a floofy paw.

"My name's Willow. You're not from around here, are you?"

"Nope," said Ted, offering his paw in return. "I'm Ted. My sister and I arrived yesterday. The big horse guy showed us a den we can stay in, and I was just collecting some wildflowers to make my bedroom pretty. Look!"

The bunny politely sniffed at what remained of Ted's flowers. But they looked a little worse for wear after Willow's attack.

"Sorry about all the kicking," said Willow.

"That's OK," said Ted cheerfully.

"Wanna play?" asked Willow.

Ted's heart gave a little leap . . . but just then he heard a roar so loud his ears flattened against his head.

"TED!"

"Uh-oh," said Ted, his tail drooping.

Nancy stormed over to the patch of grass where Ted and Willow were standing.

"Hello! I'm Willow," said Willow, offering a paw.

But Nancy ignored her completely.

"What did I say about leaving the den? GET BACK IN THE DEN."

"I was only getting us some flowers to cheer the place up!" pleaded Ted.

But Nancy just picked Ted up by the scruff

of the neck and gave him a swift kick on his bottom. Ted flew through the air and landed gracefully in the fox hole.

"She shoots, she scores!" cried Willow.

Nancy swiveled around and frowned at the young rabbit.

"Get lost, hoppy," said Nancy. "Stay away from Ted. We're not here to make friends, OK?"

Willow narrowed her eyes as Nancy strode away.

"Well, we'll see about THAT," she harrumphed. And Willow hopped away with a determined look on her face.

CHAPTER SEVEN
The grand tour

Willow did not appreciate being told what to do, especially by grumpy foxes like Nancy.

The next day, she hid in the tall grass and waited for Frank to swoop down with more Wildhorns Power Juice.

"Morning, Willow," said Frank.

"How did you see me?" said Willow, in a huff.

"Excited by our new guests, are you?" Frank smiled.

Willow pushed her nose close to Frank's

beak. Her fists were clenched and she looked extremely serious.

"I AM GOING TO MAKE THAT LITTLE FOX MY BEST FRIEND," she said through gritted teeth.

Frank chuckled.

"I don't doubt it! He'd be lucky to have a pal like you, that's for sure."

Willow produced a daisy chain from behind her back and looped it over one of the glass bottles. She gave Frank a wink before hopping over to hide in the tall grass again.

"Rise and shine, little foxes!" called Frank.

This time it was Ted who popped out of the den.

"Thank you so much, Frank!" said Ted. "Oh, it looks like another lovely day."

"You two staying inside again, then?" asked Frank.

"Nancy won't let me go anywhere," whispered Ted, pointing toward the den. "She's worried I'm going to get attacked or kidnapped or something."

Just then he spotted the daisy chain.

"Oh! Oh my goodness! How pretty," said Ted, looping it over his wrist.

"You've got an admirer," said Frank, nodding toward the tall grass.

"Thank you!" whispered Ted as loud as he dared. "Thank you so much!"

Willow's ears wiggled.

Just then Nancy crawled out of the den, grabbed a bottle, and chugged it down.

"Got any coffee in this place?" she grunted.

Frank glanced at Ted, and then at Willow, who was still hiding.

"Coffee, you say? Aye, I know just the place for coffee," he said. "Why don't you follow me?"

Nancy's ears perked up immediately.

"Awesome," she said. "Come on, Ted."

Frank swiveled his head around and gave a little cough.

"Ah, no, I'm afraid the little one will have to stay put," he said. "He's too young to be allowed where *we're* going."

Ted's tail drooped a little. He'd been hoping for at least *some* adventure. But then he noticed that the bunny ears in the tall grass were moving up and down in excitement. He looked at Frank, who had a mischievous twinkle in his eye.

"You'll be all right, Ted, right?" said Nancy. "Just stay put—I'll be back later. If I find out you've left the den, there'll be trouble . . ."

"Oh yes, that's FINE, Nance!" said Ted brightly. "You go and get your coffee. Take as long as you need."

Frank gave Ted a wink and began to glide away from the den. Nancy scampered after him.

When the coast was clear, Willow bounded out of the grass.

“Hooray!” she said. “NOW can you play?”

Ted nodded, bouncing up and down. “Yes, oh yes!”

Hey, guys, how are you doing? I've got to say, I like this Willow character. She seems **FUN!** And I'm excited about the tour. Do you think there'll be snacks? And a gift shop where I can buy a keychain? I do hope so.

Anyway, back to the story, I suppose.

Ted knew he was being a bit naughty, but no one had ever wanted to play with him before. He just had to make sure he got back to the den before Nancy.

"Why don't I give you a GRAND TOUR OF GRIMWOOD?" said Willow, clasping her paws together.

"That would be amazing!" said Ted.

"We'll start right away," said Willow, suddenly feeling very important.

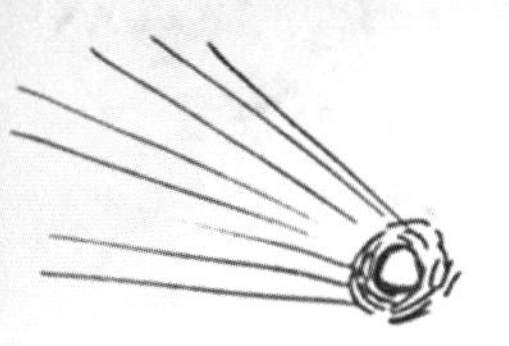

"Grimwood was discovered a gazillion and a half years ago," began Willow. "Everything was in black and white, humans hadn't been invented, and dinosaurs roamed the earth and had cars and bank accounts."

Ted scampered behind her. Willow's voice was loud and important-sounding, and she waved her paws around as she spoke, as if conducting an orchestra. She stood on top of a mound of earth and gestured toward a small pond.

“They say that this small pond is the oldest place in Grimwood,” said Willow. “We call it . . . THE SMALL POND.”

Ted looked at the small pond, which was indeed a pond, and also quite small. The water was murky, and there was a collection of upside-down shopping carts in the middle. Sitting on top of the shopping carts was a duck. She looked absolutely furious.

“That’s Ingrid,” whispered Willow. “She doesn’t like to be disturbed.”

“QUAAAAAACK!” quacked Ingrid angrily.

“How did she get all those shopping carts?” asked Ted.

“We don’t ask,” whispered Willow. “But every few months there’s another one. She takes the coins out of those little slots too, even the ones that are really jammed in. People say she’s a millionaire.”

“What? You can’t become a millionaire from stealing the coins out of shopping carts,” laughed Ted, a bit too loudly.

“QUAAAAAACK!” quacked Ingrid, sounding very angry now. “I AM a millionaire! I’ll have you know I own several hotels in Tokyo, Abu Dhabi, and New York.”

“Sorry, Ingrid!” said Willow. “It’s me, Willow. He’s new here.”

The duck stood up and wiggled her bottom. Ted noticed there were other ducks snoozing on their peculiar island of twisted-up, rusty carts.

"I used to be a great beauty, you know," cried Ingrid. "I used to be in the movies."

"Oh, how wonderful!" said Ted. "Would I have heard of any of your films?"

Ingrid plumped up her feathers. "Well . . . I had a small role in *Motorcycle Bad Guys 3*. For a few seconds you see me waddle past a policeman eating a doughnut in the park."

"That's amazing!" said Ted.

Ingrid smiled shyly. "Thank you," she said graciously. Then she stared at Ted. "Willow," she continued. "You must bring this boy to rehearsals later. We cannot waste that face."

"OK, Ingrid!" said Willow cheerfully.

"Rehearsals?" asked Ted. "For what?"

But Willow had grabbed Ted's paw and she dragged him away from the smelly pond. Soon Ted found himself walking down a trail carpeted with daffodils and daisies, until they

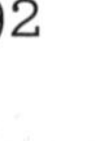

emerged upon a glorious patch of bluebells.

"And this is where I live," beamed Willow. There were bunnies *everywhere*.

"We call this part of Grimwood 'Bunnyville,'" said Willow. "But nobody knows why . . ."

"Um," said Ted. "Is it because it's a village of bunnies?"

Willow ignored him and was still looking mysteriously into the distance. "Nobody . . . absolutely nobody . . . knows why . . ."

Suddenly a low, deep grumbling sound filled the forest and shook the leaves from the trees.

"Uh-oh," said Willow. "JUMP!"

She shoved her little body into Ted, and they tumbled into the bushes.

BRRRMMMMM, BRRRRMMMMMMMM, BRRRRRMMMMMMMM!

Ted gasped as a huge open-topped car bounced past them, driven by a gang of very rowdy badgers. They were hooting and shouting at the top of their voices. One of them was guzzling something out of a large green bottle, and another one was whirling what looked like a pair of worn-out red pants around and around above its head.

"Sorry, missy!" shouted one of the badgers as the car bounced through the woods. "Didn't mean to startle you!"

"Watch where you're going, Wiggy!" shouted Willow, who looked very annoyed.

But the badgers honked the horn, so she was drowned out by a **BE-BE-BE-BEEEEEEP!**

"Troublemakers, all of them!" huffed Willow, brushing herself off and gingerly picking a nettle leaf from her paws.

Willow ushered Ted away from Bunnyville

and marched deep, deep into the forest.

Ted's neck ached as he gazed up at the trees. He'd never seen so many in his life. They were huge, gnarly things, with branches that stretched and grabbed above his head like giant claws. As he looked closer, he could see small dark shadows zooming between them.

"What are they?" he whispered.

"Squirrels, you nincompoop," said Willow. "Don't tell me you haven't seen squirrels before."

Ted had indeed seen many squirrels before. But these ones looked different. They appeared to be wearing tiny helmets and capes.

"What are they doing?" asked Ted.

"Treebonk," said Willow matter-of-factly.

"Treebonk?" said Ted. The word sounded familiar, and then he remembered that Frank had mentioned it earlier too. "What's . . ."

"Still, keeps them busy, which is useful considering the Squirrel Wars."

"The . . . Squirrel Wars?" said Ted, frowning.

"The Grimwood Squirrel Wars will probably never end," sighed Willow. "It's so annoying. There are booby traps hidden all over the place. Just last week I got caught in a net for an afternoon because I accidentally sniffed an acorn. Anyway, come on—I have to show you another amazing Grimwood thing! You won't believe your eyeballs." And Willow rushed off toward the next stop on the tour.

Hello, everyone.

I hereby present to you:

A BRIEF VISUAL HISTORY OF

SQUIRREL WARS

1800: The first red squirrels settle in Grimwood.

1800 (about half an hour later)**:** The first gray squirrels settle in Grimwood.

1845: Ethel (a red squirrel) accidentally steals a bath towel from Kenny (a gray squirrel) when they use the same clothesline.

1845 (later that afternoon)**:** Kenny hides Ethel's teabags.

1867: Small squirrels are told about the terrible Towel Incident of 1845 and the subsequent Teabag Uprising.

1867-1998: Lots of fighting.

1998: Owen (red) and Coco (gray) get married and unite the squirrels in peace and harmony.

1999: Kayleigh (gray) refuses to allow Wesley (red) to park in front of her tree.

1999-present day: The war continues, but mainly through the mediums of dance and treebonk.

CHAPTER EIGHT
Titus makes some coffee

Titus was sitting at the small table outside the camper he called home. Titus could often be found holding important mayoral meetings here, as well as late-night card games with Frank. But now, he was alone, a piece of paper in front of him, scratching his snout thoughtfully. He was trying to write a book. It was called *Memoirs of a Stag*. He'd been working on it for about three years.

"OK!" he said, sharpening his pencil. He closed his eyes and hemmed. Then he hawed.

Then he hemmed some more. He sighed. He tapped his head with the pencil. Then he said, "Ah!" and scribbled something down. He did this again and again, each "Ah!" louder than the one before. After about an hour, he set his pencil down, uttered a loud "PHEW!," and wiped his brow.

"Seven words! A good day's work," Titus said to himself, settling back into his chair to have a well-deserved nap. He was just in the middle of a delightful dream about the summer he spent fruit-picking in Italy, when the doorbell rang.

"I've brought a visitor," said Frank. "She

cheers up if you give her coffee, apparently."

Nancy grunted.

"Oh, hello, hello!" cried Titus, leaping from his armchair and clapping his hooves together. "A coffee drinker, are we? I absolutely LOVE the smell, but if I drink the stuff it wreaks havoc on my insides, just an absolute disaster. But seeing as Frank's a fan, I always keep a stash handy. Now, take a seat and settle down, young fox."

Nancy plonked herself down at the table while Frank busied himself in the camper.

Moments later he emerged with a battered pot, a couple of rusty tin cups, a carrot cake, and some cookies in his talons. He set it all down in front of Nancy and poured out the hot coffee.

Nancy inhaled deeply—*Oh, it smelled so wonderful*—and drained the cup immediately.

"Got any more?" she said, licking her lips.

Frank narrowed his eyes and poured Nancy more coffee. Then he perched on top of the camper and sipped delicately from his own cup.

"So, you're from the Big City, eh?" said Titus. "I've always wanted to visit. Tell me, is it true about the doughnut shops?"

"What about them?"

"Well . . . just that such palaces of wonder even exist! Can you really get ones covered in chocolate? And rainbow sprinkles?"

Nancy sipped her coffee a little slower this time.

"Yep. They sell them by the dozen. They're all right, I suppose."

Titus groaned.

"Such delights," he said, licking his lips. "The dark forces that drove you from the Big City must have been very serious indeed."

Nancy shuddered with pleasure as the effects of the coffee started to whoosh around her body. She relaxed into her chair a little.

"There's this cat, you see," she said. "Princess Buttons. She's a nasty piece of work. She wants to get rid of us foxes so she can have the Speedy Chicken dumpsters all to herself."

"A speedy chicken? Who *is* this terrifying bird?" asked Titus thoughtfully. "And why does it want to kill you?"

"No, the *cat* wants to kill us, not the chicken," spluttered Nancy.

"A murderous chicken," murmured Titus, ignoring Nancy completely. "You poor things."

Titus puffed out his chest.

"You and your brother will be safe from the killer chickens here," he said kindly. "And that's a Titus promise."

Nancy sighed and looked closely at Titus. He had kindly eyes, grand antlers, and big flappy nostrils. And he was clearly off his rocker.

"It's not a chicken," she repeated. "Anyway . . . we can't go back to the Big City until Princess Buttons is gone."

"And when will that be?" asked Titus.

"I don't know," said Nancy. "My friends said they'd text me to give me the all-clear. But that massive bird stole my phone, didn't she?"

Nancy was so annoyed by the memory that she banged the table with her fist, sending a sandwich cookie flying.

"Mmmm, yes," said Titus, removing the cookie from his ear and putting it into his mouth. "I am *so* sorry about Pamela stealing your phone."

Just then, the peace was shattered by a massive Jeep crashing through the forest.

BEEP, BEEP!

"COMING THROUGH!"

The badgers' Jeep bounced and clunked past Titus's camper before thunking heavily into an oak tree.

"Ow!" said the tree.

Frank flapped his wings angrily and hooted some very rude owl words that can't be repeated.

"Goodness!" said Titus, clutching his cookie to his chest.

The car was surrounded by billowing clouds of steam.

"Gnnrffghhh," said the driver, a small badger wearing a tie.

Nancy was the first to approach the Jeep and went to the driver's door.

"All right?" she said.

"Crgnrrgrg," said the badger.

Nancy helped him out. He sneezed five times and shook his head.

"Wiggy!" said Titus. "What on earth were you thinking?"

"Wah happen?!" said Wiggy.

"You hit a tree," said Nancy.

"Oh no!" said the badger, looking stricken. "Monty's going to kill me!"

Titus and Nancy helped Wiggy drag the car backward away from the tree. There was a massive dent in the hood. Nancy looked at it from a couple of angles and then leapt on top of it. She jumped twice and the hood was flat again.

"How . . . how did you do that?" gasped Wiggy.

Nancy shrugged. "Lot of cars where I'm from."

"My savior!" cried Wiggy, and he flung his arms around Nancy, who immediately pushed him away.

"Who are you?" he asked, his eyes sparkling in awe and wonder.

"One of our newest arrivals!" said Titus, beaming. "She and her little brother have only just arrived in Grimwood. Isn't that right, Nancy?"

"Yeah," said Nancy. She suddenly felt a little shy and looked at the ground.

Wiggy slapped his forehead.

"Of course!" he said. "You were the fox who was out and about with young Willow! We drove past you earlier."

Nancy frowned.

"No, you didn't," she said. "I came straight here from the den."

Frank got very still.

"HMMMMMM," said Wiggy, stroking his tie thoughtfully. "Come to think of it, this fox had big dreamy eyes and didn't seem to have your terribly scraggly ears . . . so yes, you're absolutely right, it wasn't you at all! My bad."

Nancy looked up at Frank, who was looking a little sheepish.

"Oh, come on, let the boy have some fun!" he said. "No harm will come to him here."

Nancy was fuming. "You don't KNOW that!" she barked.

"Hey guys, let's all just relax and have some carrot cake," said Titus.

Nancy pointed an angry paw at Frank. "You *knew* Ted was going to sneak off with that bunny, didn't you? Well, now you can help me find him!"

Frank swooped down to perch on Titus's antlers.

"I think," he said, opening his wings out so wide they cast a great shadow over everyone, "that someone may have forgotten their manners."

"TTRREEEEEBOOOOOOOONK!"

THWACK.

A flurry of squirrels suddenly whizzed overhead like hairy bullets.

Nancy shook her head, turned, and stomped back into the forest. Grimwood was nuts, she decided. She was going to find Ted, drag him back to the den, and sit on his head. She couldn't wait to leave this weird place.

Titus felt a little sad as he watched Nancy march away.

"She didn't even take any carrot cake with her," he sighed. "I shall have to eat it all myself."

"She reminds me of someone," said Frank, his owlish brows drawing together in a frown.

"Yes," nodded Titus, "I thought that too." And he mournfully shoveled some cake into his mouth, getting icing all over his snout.

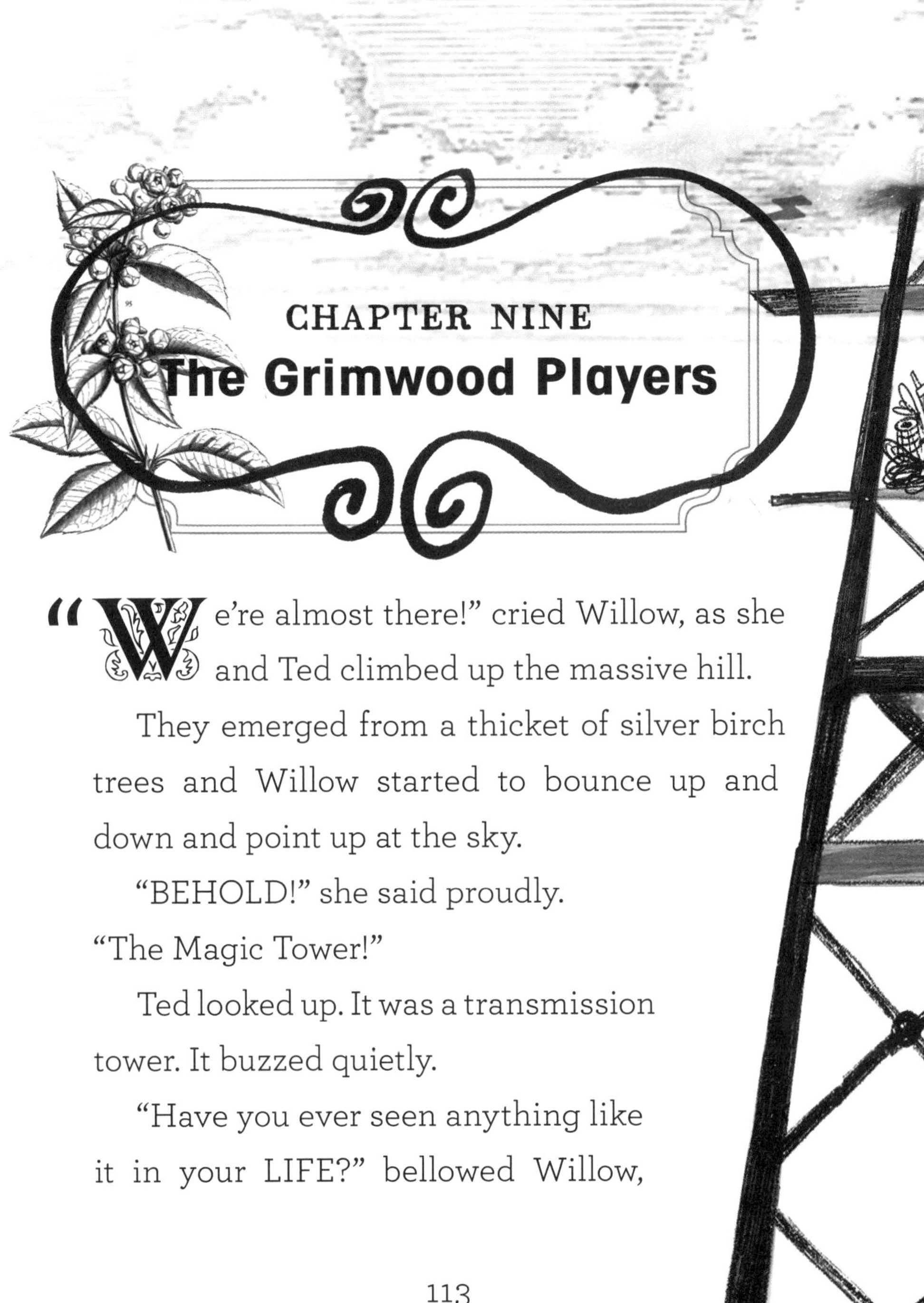

CHAPTER NINE

The Grimwood Players

"We're almost there!" cried Willow, as she and Ted climbed up the massive hill.

They emerged from a thicket of silver birch trees and Willow started to bounce up and down and point up at the sky.

"BEHOLD!" she said proudly. "The Magic Tower!"

Ted looked up. It was a transmission tower. It buzzed quietly.

"Have you ever seen anything like it in your LIFE?" bellowed Willow, still hopping up and down. “They say it gives Grimwood *magical powers*!”

Ted had, in fact, seen many transmission towers in his life. He could have told Willow that the hot, fizzy electricity flying through those cables was used by humans to watch television, charge their phones, and switch the lights on. But as he was a gentle and polite young fox, Ted just said, “No! What an amazing thing.”

Just then, a long black cable started to wave around madly in the air, like an arm made from spaghetti. There was a strange squawky noise.

“Duck!” said Ted, pushing Willow to the ground and covering their heads with his tail.

“It’s not a duck, it’s an eagle, you silly,” said Willow. “It’s Pamela. She likes to chew on the loose wire now and then. Says it gives her a ‘massive buzz.’”

"But . . . but that could KILL her!" squeaked Ted.

"Yup." Willow nodded. "But Pamela's a tough ol' bird. She wants to feel the power of the Magic Tower."

Hello, everyone! Just a friendly note to say please don't go near electricity cables, and

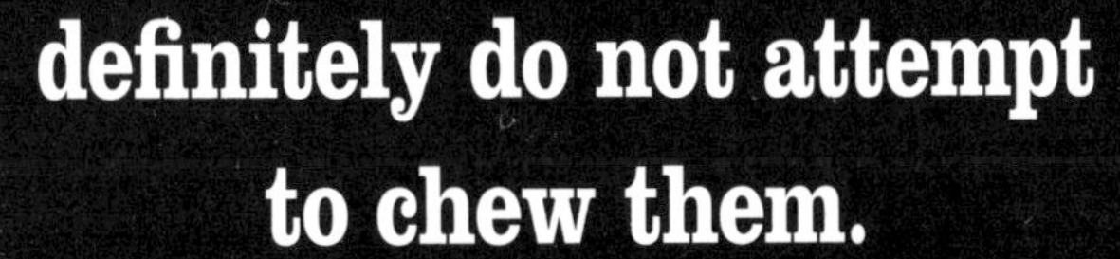

definitely do not attempt to chew them.

It would mean certain death and would likely ruin your day! Thaaaaaaanks! Xx

Ted watched as Pamela wrestled with the loose cable. He sniffed. The air stank of burning feathers.

"They say the hoomins built this tower many years ago," said Willow.

"Humans, you mean."

"Yes, hoomins. That's what I said."

"Humans."

"Hoomins."

"Humans."

"Hoomins."

"Humans."

"Hoomins."

"Humans."

"Hoomins."

Now listen, this is getting **very silly.**

"Anyway, they say that it gives Grimwood a very *special* kind of energy," said Willow.

"Oh! Is that why you're all so weird?" asked Ted.

"Pardon?"

"I mean, is that why you're all so . . . unusual?" said Ted, correcting himself.

"It's what makes us different," said Willow proudly, puffing her chest out.

Ted looked at Willow, who now seemed to be putting on some sparkly purple legwarmers. She started to stretch, making **"OOH"** and **"AAAAH"** noises as she lifted her arms, touched her toes, and wiggled her ears around.

“Just warming up before Drama Club,” she explained, bending over so much her head was between her legs. “The Big Show’s in a few days. We’ve been rehearsing for months.”

Ted clasped his paws to his face. “Drama Club? Tell me more!” he said.

“Well, every few months, there’s a big talent show in Grimwood,” said Willow.

Ted’s tail started wagging.

“What kinds of things do people do in the show?”

“Oh, all sorts,” said Willow. “The Grimwood Players put on a play or a musical. The badgers have a choir. There’s a mole called Emo Omar who recites difficult poetry.”

Ted’s brain was a-buzz with excitement.

“It sounds fantastic! Is this the rehearsal Ingrid was talking about earlier?”

"Yup," said Willow. "And she wants me to bring you. So come on, then."

There was a nagging feeling in Ted's tummy. He'd been away from the den for a while and should probably be getting back. But he pushed the feeling away.

He grabbed Willow's paw. "Let's go!"

They arrived at a grove that had been decorated with bunting and streamers. There was a small wooden stage and a few benches. Some efficient-looking beavers were adjusting two large spotlights nestled in the boughs of a pair of copper beeches. Animals were bustling around, looking very busy and important.

"Gosh!" said Ted.

Ingrid the duck's nervous-looking assistant, Tamara, waddled over to where they were standing.

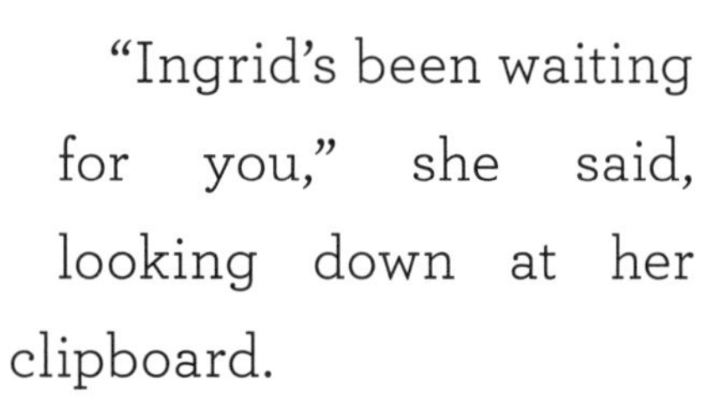

"Ingrid's been waiting for you," she said, looking down at her clipboard.

"Well, I'm here now, so everyone can relax," said Willow importantly.

"No, no, not you. *You,*" said Tamara, nodding at Ted.

Ted looked confused.

"Me?"

She herded Ted and Willow to a tree stump. Ingrid was sitting on top of it, nestled in shawls and quacking orders through a megaphone.

"There he is!" she cried, on seeing Ted. "Our new leading man!"

"What?" said Willow.

Ted's mouth hung open.

"Tell me, boy, can you act?" asked Ingrid eagerly.

Ted's mouth was still hanging open.

"Have you felt the make-up on your face melt under the hot lights?" she continued. "Soaked up the applause of an audience as you take your final bow?"

"Um . . . what's going on?" said Willow.

"Someone bit the head off our lead actor and we need a last-minute replacement," said Tamara briskly.

Willow gasped.

"Binky? Binky Snuffhausen?" she said.

Tamara nodded grimly.

"Is he . . . is he *dead*?" asked Willow.

"Yes," said Tamara. "Once his head was bitten off, that was it, really. Anyway, it's all very sad but the show must go on."

"When I saw your little face," boomed Ingrid, waddling over to cup Ted's head in her wings, "I knew, I just knew it! Look at you. Look at those eyes!"

Willow hopped up and down.

"Wow, Ted, wow! This is amazing!"

"Umm . . . but I've . . . I've never been on a stage before!" squeaked Ted.

"Then we will start your lessons at once!" cried Ingrid, clapping her wings together with delight.

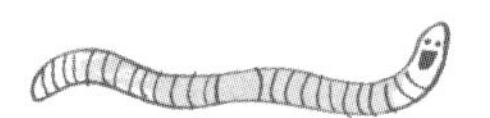

Fifteen minutes later, Ted found himself onstage. He was wearing legwarmers, a headband, and a sparkly vest. Ingrid was teaching him how to "loosen up" and make strange noises with his mouth.

"You must FEEL it rise from your stomach, up through the chest, and then PROJECT, dear boy, PROJECT!"

"OOOOOHHHhhhhhAAAAAAHHHHH!" bellowed Ted.

"Now I want you to show me joy! Show me the happiest fox on Earth," said Ingrid, waving her shawls and scarves around dramatically.

Ted thought of the happiest thing he could think of.

He laughed and skipped and bounced around the stage, picking Willow up and twirling her around and around.

"You're a natural!" said Willow.

Ted grinned and he had to admit—he loved it.

"Now show me fear," said Ingrid. "You are scared, you are alone—show me terror!"

"Argh!" he said, making his best terrified face.

Ingrid gave a quack of indignation.

"I said TERROR, boy! Let me hear your most blood-curdling scream."

Ted closed his eyes and tried to think of something really, really scary.

"AAAAUUUUAAAAAAAAAUUUURRGH!"

Ted's blood-curdling cry echoed through Grimwood.

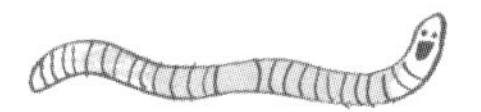

Not far away, Nancy stopped in her tracks. After much stomping and sniffing, she had finally caught Ted and Willow's scent, and she was weaving her way through the trees and bushes to find them. But hearing her little brother scream like that could only mean one thing.

"Princess Buttons!" she cried. "She's found us!"

And she ran as fast as she could to save her brother.

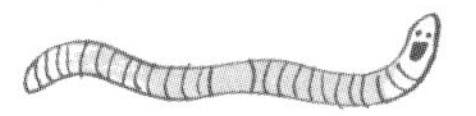

Meanwhile, Ingrid was quacking with delight and clapping her wings together.

"Again, again!" she cried.

Ted laughed and took a deep breath, before letting rip with an even louder yell.

"AAAAUUUUAAAAAAAAAUUUUURRRGH!"

Suddenly, a dark figure crashed onto the stage and leapt on Ted, throwing him to the ground and rolling him offstage.

"CUT! Stage invasion!" cried Tamara, and several security bunnies in jumpsuits hopped onto the stage.

"Nancy!" spluttered Ted.

"Are you OK?" said Nancy, her eyes wide with fear. "Is it Buttons? Where is she?"

She looked closely at Ted and patted him up and down to check that he wasn't hurt.

"I'm fine, sis!" said Ted. "I was *acting.*"

Nancy sat back and looked around her at the stage, the lights, and the other actors.

"Acting?" she spat. "ACTING?"

"Welcome to . . . the Grimwood Players!" said a small brass band of hedgehogs, who began playing a tune and tossing confetti.

"Not now, guys," said Willow.

Nancy glared at Willow before turning her attention back to Ted, who knew he was in biiiiiiig trouble.

"I told you not to leave the den," snarled Nancy. "I thought you were being ATTACKED!"

Ted whimpered and looked at the floor.

"He was just having FUN," barked Willow, who wasn't scared of Nancy AT ALL. "Remember that? Or have you always been a giant party pooper?"

Everyone gasped.

Nancy crouched down so that she was eye to eye with Willow.

"Yeah, I've always been a giant party pooper," she said. "And I've always had a taste for rabbit."

She licked her lips and bared her sharp teeth.

"Come on," she barked at Ted. "We're leaving."

And she started to drag him away by the legwarmers.

"NOW JUST ONE MINUTE, MADAME FEROCIOUS!"

came a voice through a megaphone. It was Ingrid, and she looked *very* annoyed. "You will not steal my new leading man just as soon as I have found him, oh no!"

She glared at Nancy with the eyes of a duck—and not just any old duck, but a *wronged* duck.

She nodded at Tamara, who waddled over to Ted and started dragging him back to the stage by his headband. Willow joined in.

"He's coming with ME," growled Nancy.

"No, he is staying with US!" shouted Willow.

"ME!"

"US!"

"ME!"

"US!"

"OW!" said Ted eventually. "Can you all put me down, please?"

He was dropped to the ground with a thud, and when he stood up he definitely looked a little bit longer.

"Nance," said Ted. "I'm sorry I snuck out, but I wanted to explore. And it's been amazing!"

Nancy didn't say anything.

"And, guys—listen, Nancy doesn't mean any harm. It's just . . . I don't really have a mom or dad around, so Nancy has to look after me all the time. That's why she gets so angry about things."

Willow didn't say anything, but Ingrid nodded.

"Loyalty," she said. "And strength. I respect that in a woman."

"Nancy," said Ted, suddenly sounding more grown-up than she had ever heard him before. "These guys are putting on a show and they need my help. Please will you let me join them?"

Nancy sighed. Ted looked happy, for the first time in a while.

"Please, sis," said Ted, his eyes wide. "I finally have an actual *friend*."

"Fine," said Nancy through gritted teeth. "Just don't get into trouble. I'll be checking on you."

"YIPPEE!" cried Willow, and she and Ted hugged and cheered.

GRIMWOOD
PLAYERS
with Hot New Talent
TED
Come and see
The BIG SHOW

Dear Mom and Dad

Hello! I wonder if you have come back to get us yet? A lot has happened since my last letter. We have been staying in Grimwood for a few days, and even though it is a bit weird I actually really like it! I made my first ever best friend. She is a rabbit called Willow. We are both starring in a talent show together. I wish I could draw you a map to Grimwood but Nancy ate it when we got here.

Love

Ted x

PS I have grown an extra inch!

To: Mom and Dad (Hopefully)

The Fox Den

Under the holly bush

In the huge Park

The Big City

CHAPTER TEN
Treebonkin'

Nancy went and sat by the pond. She wasn't sure what all these weird feelings were that were bouncing around inside her.

"Go away, feelings," she said. "Get lost."

And she threw an acorn into the murky water.

After a few seconds, the acorn was thrown back and it hit Nancy on the nose.

"Ow!" said Nancy and threw it back in again.

The pond threw back an even bigger acorn.

"Hey!" said Nancy, jumping to her feet. "You! Pond! Stop throwing things at me!"

"Arguing with water now, are we?" asked Frank, who was perched on the branch of a nearby hollybush. "Wouldn't surprise me."

Nancy spun around and pointed at the pond.

"Did you see that?" she barked. "That isn't normal!"

Frank shrugged.

"Lot of things aren't 'normal' around here, kid. You may as well get used to it."

Nancy gave a hollow laugh, and Frank spun his head around so it was almost backward, which is something all owls like to do now and then just to show off.

"I think I know something that might help," said Frank. "Come with me, kid."

Nancy had to run to keep up with the massive owl as he weaved his way expertly through the branches. Every now and then he had to swoop and duck as a squirrel shot overhead shouting, "TREEBONK!"

"OK, that's it," cried Nancy. "What IS treebonk? Why do I keep seeing squirrels smashing themselves into tree trunks?"

Frank chuckled.

"Treebonk is the official sport of Grimwood, and we take it *very* seriously," he said. "I remember when I first landed here, I couldn't make sense of it. But it's really very simple."

"OK, well, I'm listening," said Nancy. Frank took a deep breath and began to explain.

UM—hang on a minute! I'd actually prepared, like, a whole "thing" on treebonk. Does this mean it's not going to be used? Are you **serious?!** Look, can you at least just take a little look? You don't even have to use it in the final thing if you don't want to.

ERIC DYNAMITE'S Beginner's Guide to TREEBONK!

With additional material by

E. Dynamite

Foreword by Ericus Dynamitus

What is treebonk?

Treebonk is a game where players (or "bonkers") fling themselves into large trees. Then they must immediately bounce off that tree onto another tree, and then another, and so on, for as long as possible.

That sounds very hard.

It is.

Are you allowed to touch the ground?

Nope.

How many bonkers are on one team?

There is no limit to the number of bonkers you can have on a treebonk team. But both teams must have an equal amount of bonkers. This means there can be a great big treebonk battle with a hundred bonkers on each team. Or there can be an intense duel with bonker against bonker.

What else happens?

Players can throw off their opponents using the following methods:

Colliding in mid-air so you both crash to the ground.

Hiding in trees to tickle the armpits of the enemy.

Leaving sticky things on trunks (e.g. honey or glue) to slow down other treebonkers.

How do you win at treebonk?

The last treebonker standing wins the match.

I thought you weren't allowed to stand?

Oh, you know what I mean.

Is treebonk dangerous?

Yes.

Is treebonk stupid?

Yes.

Why are we all playing treebonk then?

There wasn't room for a tennis court.

"Right," said Nancy. "I think I understand. Is it only squirrels who play?"

"Yes," said Frank. "They're well suited to it. Big tails. Enjoy flinging themselves off trees. I coach them sometimes. I teach them about gliding. I took over after Pamela . . . after she . . . well, it doesn't matter."

At this point, three squirrels zoomed overhead and splatted against the tree boughs.

"Hi, Frank!"

"Hello!"

"Howdy!"

Frank gave the bonkers a nod as he swooped by.

Nancy shook her head. Treebonk sounded like a ridiculous game. Though she could imagine all that flying and bouncing could be kind of . . . fun.

“Ah,” said Frank after a while. “Here we are.”

Nancy looked up and saw the transmission tower.

“They call it ‘the Magic Tower,’” said Frank.

“It’s a transmission tower,” said Nancy flatly.

“Yes, I know, smartypants,” said Frank. “It certainly *used* to be. But now . . . well, now it’s a little bit more than that.”

And he swooped down, grabbed Nancy by the scruff of the neck, and flew high into the air.

"AAAAAARRRGH!" said Nancy.

Frank gently lowered her onto a small wooden plank.

“Don’t look down.”

Nancy gulped. She wasn’t generally scared of heights. But the Magic Tower was taller than any wall or roof she’d been on in the Big City.

““W-wh-why are we here?” she gasped.

“Thought you might want your phone back,”

said Frank. "Didn't you say your friends in the city were going to text you?"

Nancy very carefully turned around and saw what looked like a massive bird's nest. It was piled high with wires, plugs, computers, and *lots* of cell phones.

"Wow," said Nancy.

Frank circled the nest a couple of times.

"Pamela!" he called. But there was no reply.

"Hmm," said Frank. "Now what does your phone look like?"

"Sort of . . . phone-y," said Nancy. She was standing very still. Any sudden movement and she knew she could plummet to the ground and land with a splat.

"Maybe we can ask Pamela," said Frank.

"ASK PAMELA WHAT?" said Pamela, poking her head up from a pile of wires and broken gadgets. She was wearing a weird helmet that beeped and buzzed and flashed.

"Pamela," said Frank. "We were just looking for you."

"I'm recording a podcast," she said, gesturing at the headphones clamped to her head.

"Can I have my phone back? You know, the one that you stole?" said Nancy.

"No," said Pamela.

"Why not?" said Frank.

"Because I ate it," said Pamela.

Nancy slapped her forehead in despair.

"Oh, Pamela," said Frank.

Pamela rummaged around in her piles of electrical junk. Eventually she held up a piece of smashed-up phone screen, with a few wires sticking out of the back.

"This is all that's left," said Pamela. "But I need it! It's a tracking device. For when the aliens arrive."

"What aliens?" asked Nancy.

Pamela's eyes grew big and started swirling around like ping-pong balls in a washing machine.

"THE ALIENS!" she shouted, waving her wings around and generally looking unhinged. "They will be here SOON! They want to destroy us. We must be ready for attack!"

Nancy sighed.

"Forget it, Frank," she said. "Can you take me back to the den, please?"

Frank gave Pamela a very stern look.

"I think you owe our little fox friend an apology," he said.

"SORRY!" squawked Pamela. Then she stuck her tongue out at Frank and flew off.

Back in the den, Nancy sighed as she watched Frank fly away. She was going to have to get in touch with Bin and Hedge some other way. She had hoped they would be able to defeat Princess Buttons together, but now it looked like she needed to think up another plan. Lost in thought, she scraped her claw along the wall of the den, scratching out her name, like she used to do in the Big City.

As she added the "y" with a final flourish, there was a CLUMP. She looked down at the clod of earth by her feet and realized she'd dislodged a chunk of wall.

"Oops," she said. But then she noticed something peculiar.

Her scraping had exposed a large slab of smooth, gray stone.

And in the middle of the stone were two faded paw prints. One was slightly bigger than the other. Nancy ran her paw softly over them.

"Huh," she said.

If she held her paw directly over the smaller print, it seemed to fit perfectly.

"Weird," she whispered.

She sniffed at the stone but couldn't pick up any particular scent. They must have been made some time ago.

Nancy lay back on her bunk. There was something about Grimwood. She couldn't quite put her finger on it, but it was making her feel . . . odd. She poked at Princess Buttons's tail, which dangled over her head.

She needed to get rid of Princess Buttons once and for all, so that she and Ted could safely return home.

Does anyone have any ideas? **Anything?**

You at the back, there? Nope.

Sorry. We're all out.

CHAPTER ELEVEN
Tails of the city

Heyyyy, Dynamite fans! Now we're going to whoosh miles and miles away from Grimwood and head back to the Big City! You'd forgotten all about that place, hadn't you? Anyway, you find out what's going on while I head to the store to stock up on cookies and bananas.

Byeeeee!

Princess Buttons knew that she looked absolutely ridiculous without a tail. It was a very difficult thing to replace.

But, most of all, she hated looking WEAK. She knew that Ted biting off her tail was still the talk of the Speedy Chicken dumpsters.

"Those foxes must be found," she hissed at nobody in particular. "And then they must be DESTROYED!" She banged the top of the green dumpster with her fist.

"O-kaaaaaaaaay," said a rat called Kelvin, who really didn't want to get involved and backed away slowly.

Just then, a member of her evil cat gang, Denise, trotted over looking very pleased with herself.

"I think I know how we can get to them, Miss Buttons," she said.

"How?" said Princess Buttons, clutching Denise by the neck and shaking her back and forth. "HOW?"

"Aarrrargh! All right, calm down. Um, well, those two other foxes. Their idiot friends. I know where they are," said Denise, who now felt less interested in helping Princess Buttons, what with the whole being-grabbed-by-the-neck thing.

Princess Buttons let go of Denise and held a flashlight under her face. She made her voice deep and growly.

"Take me to the foxes—NOW!"

"What"s the magic word?" said Denise, who believed basic manners were important.

"OR ELSE I WILL KILL YOU," said Princess Buttons.

Denise decided it was best just to get on with it.

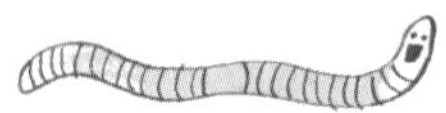

Bin and Hedge were lounging around in Ted and Nancy's old fox den in the park.

"I really miss her," said Bin, chewing thoughtfully on a stick. "She was the first fox I ever met. In fact, she gave me my name."

"No way!" said Hedge. "She gave me my name too. Because she found me in a hedge."

"No way!" said Bin. "She found me in a garbage bin."

The foxes high-fived each other. They had been avoiding the Speedy Chicken dumpsters ever since that fateful night, when Ted bit Princess Buttons's tail off.

"Has she texted you yet?" said Hedge.

"Nah," said Bin. "But I'll message her as soon as we know if that mean old cat Buttons is still sniffing around."

There was a knock at the den, which was weird because it didn't really have a door.

"Pizza delivery!" shouted someone (can you guess who?).

"Come in!" said Hedge.

The hedge opened—

—and the foxes came face to face with . . .

PRINCESS BUTTONS! And her smelly and horrible evil cat gang were right behind her, looking ready to have a big fight or say mean stuff or something.

"Hey . . . you're not a pizza," shouted Bin.

"No, I'm not," hissed Princess Buttons. "I am a very angry cat whose tail was murdered by YOUR friends."

"I would have preferred pizza," said Bin.

"Where are they? Your nasty little fox pals?" said Princess Buttons.

"We don't know," said Hedge. "Look, you've

got the stupid dumpsters all to yourselves. Why don't you leave us alone?"

Just then, Bin's phone pinged.

"Ooh, I wonder if it's Nancy!" said Bin. "We've been waiting for them to get in touch, haven't we Hedge?"

Hedge smacked herself on the forehead.

Princess Buttons looked at the phone. Bin looked at the phone. Hedge looked at the phone.

"Attack!" yelled Princess Buttons.

In the kerfuffle, Princess Buttons managed to grab Bin's phone and squeeze her way out of the den. Denise was waiting outside with the getaway vehicle.

"This is gold—gold, I tell you!" shrieked Princess Buttons.

"Where are we going?" asked Denise, pushing the skateboard as fast as her paws could manage.

"We're going to visit the most dangerous mouse in the entire world," said Princess Buttons.

"Fine," said Denise, because what else was she going to say? Princess Buttons paid her salary after all, plus the school year was coming up and the kids needed shoes.

The most dangerous mouse in the entire world worked in a tiny secret mouse laboratory underneath a much bigger secret human laboratory. Her name was Dr. Fairybeast.

Dr. Fairybeast used her amazing brain and scientific powers for both good and evil. It really depended on her mood. On the first day

Princess Buttons turned up to Dr. Fairybeast's secret lab, the arrow on the Fairybeast-o-meter was pointing toward "Good." And, sure enough, inside the lab, Dr. Fairybeast was using complicated math to heal old people's knees, and had invented some felt tip pens that never ran out of ink.

But the day after *that*, the arrow was pointing at "Evil," so Princess Buttons walked straight in and, indeed, there was Dr. Fairybeast looking wicked and burning ants with a magnifying glass.

"I've got a job for you, Dr. Fairybeast," said Princess Buttons. She handed over Bin's phone.

"I need you to find someone. Their number will be stored in this phone. Can you do it?"

Dr. Fairybeast snorted.

"Of course," she said. "This will be simple. I will plug the phone into my satellite geolocator machine thing, press a few buttons, and it will be done."

"Hooray!" said Princess Buttons. "That was easy."

Dr. Fairybeast lowered her glasses. "But it will cost you," she said.

"Anything!" said Princess Buttons. "Anything at all!"

Dr. Fairybeast walked over to a tiny filing cabinet inside a matchbox. She pulled out a piece of paper.

“You must bring me all of the items on this list. Failure to do so means I will have to do unspeakably awful and evil things to you.”

Princess Buttons looked at the list.

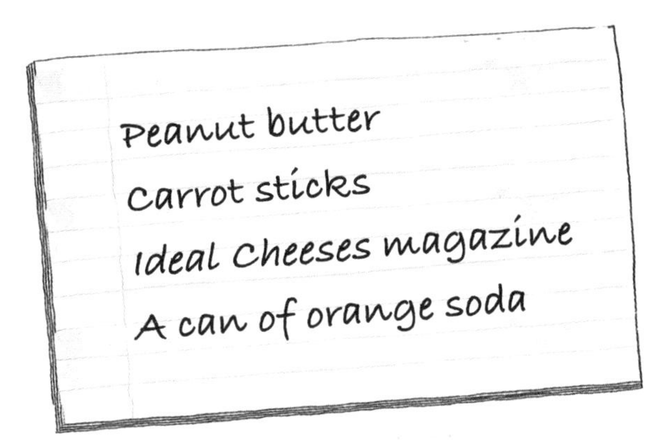
Peanut butter
Carrot sticks
Ideal Cheeses magazine
A can of orange soda

“If you can search this city high and low, and get these sacred items to me by 5 p.m. *sharp* . . . then and only then can I begin the search for your . . . friend.”

Princess Buttons looked at her watch.

"There's a corner store just down the road, I'll be back in a sec," she said.

Princess Buttons and Denise went to the corner store, and they bought:

PEANUT BUTTER
CARROT STICKS
IDEAL CHEESES MAGAZINE
A can of ORANGE SODA

And Denise also bought:

Some CHEESY PUFFS
Some of those CANDIES that look like pacifiers
A PACKET OF TISSUES, because they always come in handy and you can never have too many.

==============================
TILL 1

"Oh, that was quick," said Dr. Fairybeast when they returned.

She took Bin's phone and connected it to the big bleepy computer thing.

"What's the name of your victim, uh, I mean friend?" asked Dr. Fairybeast.

"Nancy," growled Princess Buttons.

"Ah, yes . . . here we go," said Dr. Fairybeast.

Nancy's phone number popped up on the screen.

"Do we call her?" asked Princess Buttons. "To see where she is?"

"No, you idiot," said Dr. Fairybeast. She typed lots of things into the computer, and the screen went fuzzy. It turned into a map. Then a little red dot appeared in the top left-hand corner.

"There she is," said Dr. Fairybeast.

They zoomed in on the map.

"Looks like they're in the countryside," said Dr. Fairybeast with a shudder.

"Not for long," said Princess Buttons, rubbing her paws together. "I'm coming to get you, little foxes! And I want my tail back! Muahahahahahahahahhahaaaaaa!"

"You're not going to *hurt* these little foxes, are you?" asked Dr. Fairybeast. "Because if you are I'll feel awful. I may be evil, but I'm not *that* evil."

"Not at all!" said Princess Buttons.

"OK," said Dr. Fairybeast, and she handed back Bin's phone. "This phone is now a Fox Finder. Switch it on and it will show you the map, and also the location of this Nancy."

"Oh, one more thing," said Princess Buttons. "You don't happen to have any kind of terrible device hanging around, do you? Something that could zap someone into thin air."

Dr. Fairybeast thought about it.

"You're definitely not going to hurt the little foxes, right?" she asked.

"Oh, absolutely not, no way," said Princess Buttons, licking her paw nonchalantly.

Dr. Fairybeast quietly pushed the arrow on the Fairybeast-o-meter all the way over to "Extra Evil!".

Then she scampered over to a very large cupboard and came back carrying a large contraption.

It was a green metal helmet with three long antennae sticking out of it. She plonked it on the floor.

"Behold! The Brain Zapper 3000!" she cried.

"Oooh!" said Denise and Princess Buttons.

"It's an extremely powerful, dangerous machine," said Dr. Fairybeast. "I'm very proud of it."

"How does it work?" asked Princess Buttons.

"You strap it to your head and when the time is right, press this red button. A powerful laser beam will shoot out of one of the antennae and fry your opponent like an egg!"

"Oooooh!" said Denise and Princess Buttons again.

"But beware. It's fully charged with forty-five million megavolts of electricity. So I'm afraid you can only use it three times."

"That's fine," said Princess Buttons. "I only need to use it twice. How much is it?"

Dr. Fairybeast thought some more.

"It'll cost you a lifetime supply of Speedy Chicken doughnuts."

"It's a deal," said Princess Buttons.

And the villains danced around Dr. Fairybeast's secret lair, cackling and generally being terrible.

CHAPTER TWELVE
The swamp

Ted was giddy with excitement. The Grimwood Players would be meeting soon for a final dress rehearsal before the Big Show later that night.

"You're going to come and watch me, aren't you, sis?" he said, bouncing up and down in the den.

Nancy drained the last of her coffee.

"Yeah," she grunted. "Got nothing better to do, do I?"

He ran over to her and flung his arms around her waist.

"Wish me luck, Nance!"

"Break a paw, kid," she said and gently ruffled the fur between his ears.

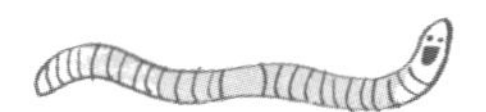

After Ted had gone to rehearsal, Nancy went to her side of the den and removed the blanket she had thrown over the mysterious paw prints. She hadn't told Ted about her discovery. She ripped out a blank sheet of paper from his notebook and found half a crayon. She traced the paw prints onto the paper. Then she ripped Princess Buttons's tail from the wall and stuffed it into her jacket pocket. It suddenly felt risky leaving it just hanging on the wall, and something in Nancy's gut was telling her that trouble was around the corner . . .

No, it's not trouble,

actually, it's just me, your friend and neighbor Eric B. Dynamite.

Back at the rehearsal, Willow was talking to Ted about the special dance they were going to perform at the very end of the Big Show.

"You'll be fine," she assured him. "Just do everything I do, but backward."

They were practicing their dance moves backstage, while various crew hurried around with spotlights and microphones. Ingrid's assistant, Tamara, was wearing sunglasses and shaking uncontrollably. There had been an awful lot for her to organize.

Some rabbits had permanently vanished during the magic act. Emo Omar said he was "too emotional" to recite any of his poetry. The badgers, meanwhile, were practicing their singing, which was *so* terrible that even the nearby flowers started crying.

"It's going to be a disaster!" wailed Tamara. "You two kids better not let me down."

Willow gave a salute. "I promise we will be fabulous," she said. "Ted and I have been practicing every day."

Tamara waddled away, muttering to herself.

Ted suddenly looked terrified.

"Willow . . . what if I'm terrible?" he said.

But Willow just shrugged. "Let's have fun dancing around and don't worry about anything else. Something crazy *always* happens. Last year someone set fire to a squirrel. Is your sister coming?"

"Oh yes, she said she would," beamed Ted.

"Really?" said Willow. "I thought this kind of thing would be too cheerful for someone as miserable as her."

Ted frowned.

"She just misses her friends and the Big City, I think," he said. "Maybe if . . . maybe if *some* people were a bit *nicer* to her, she wouldn't be so grumpy."

"By 'some people' do you mean me?" asked Willow.

"Yes." Ted grinned. "Please could you try? I think you and Nancy actually have a lot in common."

Willow frowned and stomped off for a coffee break, which proved Ted's point entirely.

When Nancy arrived at Titus's camper, she found him wrapped in a ratty red robe, rolling around on the floor.

"What are you doing?" she asked.

"Oh! Hello there. Just ironing my mayoral robe!" said Titus, slowly getting up and dusting himself off.

Nancy took the sheet of paper out of her pocket.

"Who do these paw prints belong to?" she asked.

Titus trotted over to take a closer look. "Hmm . . . they don't ring any bells. Where are they from?"

"I found them in the den. Painted onto a lump of stone."

"Well, they belong to a pair of foxes, I'd say," he said.

"You've been in Grimwood forever. You must know whose they are!" said Nancy.

Titus shrugged. "There are many creatures in Grimwood who I know, and many that I don't. And there are some who I may have simply forgotten all about."

Nancy growled and shoved the paper back in her pocket.

"Who do you *want* those paw prints to belong to, young Nancy?" asked Titus gently.

Nancy looked at the floor.

"I can't remember them," she said slowly.

"Who?"

"My parents. I can't remember them."

Titus and Nancy sat in silence for some time.

"Well. That's a difficult thing for young shoulders to carry," said Titus eventually. "But you carry it very well, Nancy. I don't know who your parents were or where they are now. But I know they taught you well. They would be very proud of how you look after your brother."

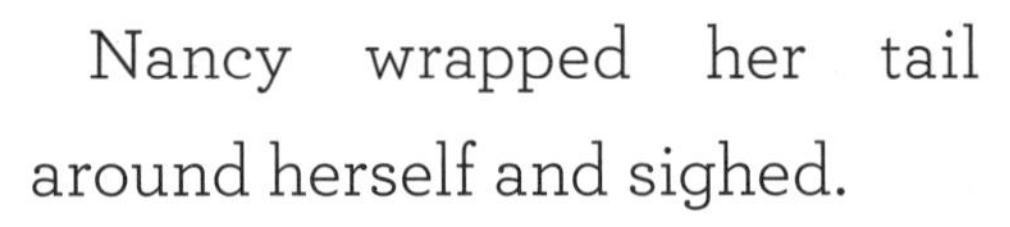

Nancy wrapped her tail around herself and sighed.

"I don't know why, but I've just got this *feeling*," she said. "It feels like they're near me. I didn't have this feeling in the Big City, but I've got it here."

Titus smiled. "Young Ted has certainly made himself at home, hasn't he? Does he miss the Big City too?"

"I dunno. Not really."

"Did he have many friends there?" asked Titus.

"No," said Nancy, which was something she hadn't really thought about before. "I suppose he didn't."

"Now you must excuse me, Nancy," said Titus. "I have important mayoral stuff to do. See you at the show later!"

Nancy grunted and stomped back off toward the den. She felt foolish for talking to Titus about the paw prints. And she couldn't shake the feeling that something was off.

"I'm gonna have to go back to the city and sort that cat out myself," she vowed.

There had been no word from Bin and Hedge so she would have to do it alone. At least she knew Ted would be safe with his new friends. She'd wait until after the show to tell him about her plan.

Suddenly a voice called out from through the trees.

“Nancy!”

Nancy’s fur stood on end.

“Nancy, where are you?”

“Who are you?” shouted Nancy. She didn’t recognize the voice, but she couldn’t just ignore it. She crept warily toward the sound, but the ground was covered with ivy and sticks that cracked and rustled as she moved.

“I miss pavement,” she grumbled. After a while the sharp twigs and wiry tendrils gave way to softer ground and Nancy breathed a sigh of relief.

“Nancy!” came the voice again. “I can’t see you!”

“I’m coming!” shouted Nancy.

Gray clouds gathered and strong winds started to whip through the trees. As Nancy continued, the ground beneath her feet began to feel swampy and sticky. Her paws glooped and slooped their way slowly through the mud. The rain got heavier and Nancy started to shiver. Every time she put her foot down, it seemed to sink a little deeper.

Gloop. Sloop. Ploop.

She needed a stick, maybe . . . something to stop her from . . .

Gloop. Ploop. Sloop.

. . . getting stuck, because the mud was so sticky and . . .

Gloop.

As long as it didn't go over her knees . . .

Sloop.

Oh no.

Ploop.

Nancy looked around. She was in the middle of a swamp and she was sinking. Fast.

"AAAAAAAARGH!"

In the nick of time, Nancy managed to yank some ivy from the base of a fallen tree. She held on to it for dear life. After a few seconds, she tied it around her waist. But she knew that if it snapped, the swamp would suck her down like a pea in a drain.

"Nancy?"

came the mysterious voice, which sounded closer than ever.

"Nancy? Is that you? Ribbit."

Nancy looked up and saw that the voice belonged to . . . a frog. Who was perched on a log.

"Who . . . who are you?" she panted.

"Oh, hello! Me? Why, my name's Gavin. Who are you? Ribbit."

"I'm Nancy! You . . . you were calling me?"

The frog looked confused.

"I don't think I was," said Gavin.

Then *another* frog hopped over, carrying grocery bags.

"Sorry, love," it said. "The lines were an absolute nightmare."

"Nancy!" cried Gavin. "You'll never guess what? See that fox down there, close to drowning in that swamp? Her name's Nancy too!"

"No way!" said Nancy the frog.

"Way!" said Gavin.

“Could you help me, please?” asked Nancy the fox.

But Gavin and Nancy the frog had already hopped away, because it was their wedding anniversary and they were going to the movies.

Hmm, I wonder what Gavin and Nancy were going to see?

"Help!" shouted Nancy. "HELP!"

But apart from the howl of the wind and the patter of the rain, Nancy was all alone.

CHAPTER THIRTEEN
The Princess and the Brain Zapper

The storm raged over Grimwood. The efficient-looking beavers were zooming around covering up the lights and props for the Big Show. Ingrid was telling the performers stories of opening night disasters from her past, while Tamara was lying face down in a puddle.

"Ooh, dear," said Ted, peeking from behind a curtain. "It's not looking good, is it?"

Willow giggled and did a backflip.

"I love storms," she said. "It makes *everything* more dramatic."

Nancy, who was still stuck in a massive swamp, definitely did *not* like storms. In the Big City, storms meant sneaking under cars and hiding out under bus stops. It didn't mean shaking and shivering and being covered in gloopy mud.

"HELP!" she yelled.

It wasn't a word she was very used to saying. But there was no way she was going to be able to get out of this pickle by herself. Then Nancy noticed a strange flash of light on the trees above her. She sniffed the air. Gasoline! And was that low rumble coming from an engine? It must be the badgers. *Phew!* thought Nancy. She was about to call out again . . . when she heard a horribly familiar voice.

"Is this it? Eww, what an absolute *dump* . . ."

Nancy's blood froze. It was Princess Buttons. And, by the sound of it, she wasn't alone. She tried to crane her neck to see.

"Yep, this is it," said another voice. "Well, as close as I can get the car. See the flashing red dot over there? That's where Nancy is."

There was some murmuring and rustling. Nancy tried to figure out how many cats there were, but it was impossible to tell. She heard a strange beeping sound and another cat's voice, one she didn't recognize.

"It's saying we need to go that way . . . toward that massive *thing*," said the cat.

"It's a transmission tower," said someone else.

"Who's got the Brain Zapper 3000?" barked Princess Buttons.

Nancy gulped. The Brain Zapper 3000? That didn't sound good.

"It's in the trunk," said another voice.

And then Nancy saw her. Princess Buttons had trotted over to the other side of the car.

"Strap it to my head," ordered Princess Buttons. "I can't wait to zap those foxes into smithereens!"

Nancy gulped again, watching as one of the cats attached a large green metal helmet to Princess Buttons's small, angry head. Then Princess Buttons pressed a switch on the side of the helmet. It began to hum and whirr, and little lights flashed at the ends of three metal antennae.

"Three zaps!" hooted Princess Buttons. "That should be enough to get rid of the pair of them."

Then something made her stop in her tracks. It was a poster nailed to a tree.

"Hang on. What's this?" she said, tearing it off. "That's him!" she said. "The fox! The little devil who bit off my tail!"

"Oh yeah!" said another voice. "He looks much smaller in real life, doesn't he?"

Nancy's heart sank.

"Right," said Princess Buttons, rubbing her paws together. "Here's the plan. You all head to this . . . 'BIG SHOW.' Grab the fox. Then bring him to me."

"Where will you be?" asked a voice Nancy didn't recognize (it was Denise, though).

Princess Buttons pointed to the Magic Tower.

"I'll be there. Bring him to me alive. I want his sister to watch me laser him to smithereens!"

And she patted the Brain Zapper 3000.

"Right!" said Denise, clapping her paws together. "You heard her, everyone. Let's kidnap the cute little foxy."

It took every last bit of strength Nancy had not to shout "NO!", but she knew she had to stay quiet. She heard the cats heading deeper into Grimwood, on their way to kidnap her brother. For the first time in her life, Nancy had no way to save him.

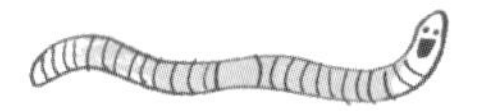

After what had felt like forever, the wind died down and the rain slowed to a drizzle. With no time to lose, the very efficient beavers started to uncover the stage for the Big Show.

Tamara had pulled herself together, and Ingrid was fluttering around backstage giving last-minute advice to the performers.

"Oh, doesn't it all look wonderful, Frank?" said Titus, clapping his hooves together as the audience started to take their seats.

"Indeed." Frank nodded, though he preferred to listen to complicated jazz music in the privacy of his own living room.

"But where's Nancy?" said Titus. "We had a very good talk earlier. I think she's quite fabulous, you know."

"Yes, she's a toughie," said Frank. "I know one when I see one."

Slowly the audience grew, until it seemed like all of Grimwood was there.

Ted was pacing up and down behind the curtain.

"Calm down!" said Willow. "You're making *me* nervous."

"I've got butterflies in my tummy," moaned Ted.

"Why did you eat butterflies?" gasped Willow.

"No, I just mean I'm nervous! Can you see the audience?"

Willow poked her nose out and had a peek.

"Yup," she said.

"Is Nancy there?" asked Ted.

"Nope," said Willow.

"Oh." Ted's tail drooped.

"But listen, Ted," said Willow. "Titus *is* there. And so is Frank. And so is Ingrid, and Tamara . . . *all* of the bunnies, and the rest of the Grimwood Players. And they're all looking forward to the show. They're all here to see us!"

Ted smiled. His friend was right.

Ingrid took the stage to introduce the first act, and the crowd began to clap and hoot in anticipation. First up was Emo Omar . . .

I move soil with my paws
As I dig
Dig dig dig
Dig down into the mysterious earth

Will I ever find
What I am looking for?
In the darkness
Oh, the darkness

Oh yes there it is
My keychain
With a picture of a unicorn on it
What a result.
(FIN)

Frank was still bobbing his owlish head around looking for Nancy. Something didn't feel right.

"Nancy said she'd be here, didn't she? I'm going to go search for her," he murmured to Titus, and quietly swooped away. He knew the woods as well as anyone, so after a quick check of the fox den, he circled high, high, high up in the air, his beady eyes scanning the ground beneath him for anything unusual.

The first thing he noticed was a car. It wasn't the badgers' Jeep, that was for sure. But as he flew closer to investigate, he saw Nancy's tired head poking out of the swamp. Though she was still holding on to the ivy, most of her body had sunk down into the awful blackness. Her eyes were closed.

"Nancy!" shouted Frank. He hovered in front of her face and tried to tickle her nose with his feathers. He didn't dare try to land—he'd sink immediately.

"Wake up, girl!"

Nancy opened her eyes.

"Frank?" she said, her voice hoarse from shouting.

"You hang on," said Frank. "I'm getting help. We're getting you out of here."

"Princess Buttons," croaked Nancy. "She's here."

But Frank had already zoomed away.

Nancy wasn't sure if it was ten minutes or ten

hours later, but the next thing she remembered was feeling a length of rope being tied firmly around her. Then she heard Frank shout, "Drive, Wiggy, drive!"

She felt hot exhaust fumes belch all over her as Wiggy got the Jeep into gear and rolled it forward, pulling her slowly out of the gloop.

"You poor thing!" said Wiggy, getting out of the car and helping her up.

Nancy felt dizzy and heavy, and held on firmly to Wiggy.

"Where's Ted?" she asked him as he removed the rope from her waist.

"He's onstage! The Grimwood Players are halfway through the play. He's absolutely *marvelous*."

Nancy and Wiggy jumped into the Jeep.

"Ted's in danger," she said.

"What happened? Is it that cat?" asked Frank.

Nancy nodded. "Buttons is here and she's not alone. But I think I've got a plan."

Frank stood at attention.

"What can I do?"

"Head to the Magic Tower and I'll meet you there. But first, I need to get to Ted before the cats do," said Nancy. "Wiggy, how fast can you go?"

Wiggy revved the engine and lowered his driving goggles.

"Hold on tight," he growled. "And GET READY FOR THE RIDE OF YOUR LIFE."

(He'd always wanted to say something like that.)

Oooh, ooh, ooh, a plan is afoot, a plan is afoot! I can feel it in my exoskeleton!

CHAPTER FOURTEEN
Attack!

The Grimwood Players were halfway through their second act. Willow was in the middle of her grand speech.

"Because I realize, Mr. Hathersage, that it is you I have loved all along. From the moment I saw you, I knew that we were going to be together, forever!"

And then she collapsed dramatically into Ted's arms.

"Aaah!" said the audience.

"ATTACK!" came a cry from the darkness. As if from nowhere, an army of cats rose from the undergrowth and ran toward the stage.

There were gasps and screams from the audience, except Titus, who clapped his hooves together and said, "Ooh, ooh, is this part of the show?"

The cats leapt onto the stage and pinned Ted and Willow to the floor. This was *not* part of the show.

"Oh, shoot," said Ted.

Willow was thumping cats away with her hind legs, but there were just too many of them.

"Take the fox to the transmission tower!" shouted Denise, who had grabbed Willow by the ears.

"HEY! You're not taking anyone anywhere," said Willow, kicking Denise in the face.

Denise growled. She flexed her claws and prepared to give Willow's face a scratching . . .

"NO!" shouted Ted. "Leave the bunny alone! It's me you want, not her."

And Ted gingerly stood up, with two cats holding his paws firmly behind his back.

"Fine," said Denise. She let go of Willow, who flopped to the floor, and grabbed Ted instead.

"You can't do this!" quacked Ingrid. "He's

part of the closing act! You'll be hearing from my agent!"

A cat hissed and swiped at her turban.

As the feral felines swarmed the stage, Titus knew he needed to do something. When

Grimwood was being attacked, it was up to him to defend it.

He stood up, closed his eyes, and took a deep breath.

"TREEBONK!"

he bellowed.

Until now, the Grimwood animals had mostly been frozen in shock. But with Titus's rallying call, they knew what to do. Almost without thinking, they scampered to the trees. And then a hundred cries of "TREEBONK!" filled the air.

They began to fling themselves off the branches.

"Treeeeeeebonk!"

They zoomed through the sky.

"Treeeeebooooooonk!"

The cats who were holding Ted dropped him and ran for cover. Ted looked over and found Willow.

"You saved me!" she cried, throwing her arms around him and untying his paws. "Now, quick, start treebonking before you get caught again."

"But I don't know how to treebonk!" said Ted.

"Just bounce around the trees as fast as you can and try not to hit the ground. GO!" shouted Willow. "TREEEEEEBOOOOOOONK!"

Ted grabbed onto a nearby pine tree and clambered up it, going as high as he could. He tried very hard not to think about how scared of heights he was. Animals were flying past his nose at high speeds, and Princess Buttons's cat gang looked very confused.

But then one of them—a big, snarly one with half an ear—spotted Ted nestled in the pine tree.

"The fox!" it yelled, "I see him!"

And the cat started to climb up the tree trunk.

Ted gulped. It was now or never.

"TREEEEBONK!" he shouted, and leapt as high in the air as he could manage. He was about to collide with a silver birch, and put his tail out to cushion the fall—and then he joyfully BOINGED off it.

"Treebonk!" he cried again, using his tail to push off the second tree and . . . it worked! His big, bushy, foxy tail turned out to be the perfect treebonking paddle. The animals of Grimwood thwacked into as many of the cats as they could manage, while boinging and twirling and spinning through the air. Not all of them were natural treebonkers—it was a squirrel thing, really. And yet, it was like a beautiful, extremely dangerous furry ballet.

"Treeebooooooonk!"

The cats were terrified. They yowled in panic and ran for cover. Acorns, branches, and squirrels rained down on them, and the cats realized they were greatly outnumbered.

Denise looked at her watch. If they piled into the car and drove without stopping, the cats could be back in the Big City by dinnertime.

"Retreat!" she shouted. "Retreat!"

Titus banged together two halves of a coconut shell, as was tradition at the end of every game of treebonk.

"TREEBONKIUS CONSUMMAVI!" he cried.

The treebonking slowed, and then stopped, until the only noise that could be heard was the quiet thud of concussed squirrels falling to the ground.

At that moment Wiggy's Jeep crashed through the trees.

"TED!" barked Nancy, leaping out of the passenger seat before Wiggy had time to stop. She ran over to Titus.

"Where is he?" she cried.

"Oh, dear Nancy, look at you!" said Titus. "I take it you found the Swamp of Despair?"

"Nancy!" cried Ted, scrambling out of a bramble bush. "Where did you go?"

"Buttons is here," they both said at exactly the same time.

"She went to the Magic Tower," said Nancy.

"It's only a matter of time before she finds us, Nance," said Ted.

"I'm gonna knock her head off!" said Willow, punching her palm.

"No," said Nancy calmly. "I've got an idea. But, Ted, I'm gonna need you. And you're going to have to be really, *really* brave."

Ted shook the twigs and acorns from his fur.

"I can do that." He grinned.

Fig 2: Blodwyn
The Slug

CHAPTER FIFTEEN
The Magic Tower

The Brain Zapper 3000 weighed heavily on Princess Buttons's head. Making it to the top of the hill was difficult for a cat who had eaten as many Speedy Chicken nuggets as she had that morning.

"Almost . . . there," she panted. She glanced at the Fox Finder. She was close to the flashing red dot. Nancy was around here somewhere.

After more huffing and puffing, Princess Buttons reached the top of the hill. She slumped against the base of the old transmission tower and waited for the cats to deliver Ted.

They *must* have him by now, the weedy little thing. She gazed up at the sky and saw two birds gliding overhead—larger than the ones in the Big City, but too far away to be of much interest.

Then she heard the unmistakable rumble of a car engine. This was it! She giggled to herself as she stood up and switched on the Brain Zapper 3000. It hummed and the antennae began to flash and glow.

A Jeep zoomed over the brow of the hill, skidding into a turn.

"DELIVERY!"

A small sack was thrown out of the window, landing near Princess Buttons's feet.

"MMmppppph!" said the bundle, which writhed and wriggled.

Princess Buttons was just about to open the sack when it was torn apart from inside. Ted's snout poked out, gasping for air.

"AAAAAAARGH!" he cried, seeing Princess Buttons and the Brain Zapper 3000.

"Finally," sighed Princess Buttons. Though she also wondered why Denise and the cats hadn't stopped the car.

"H . . . hello," said Ted nervously.

"Where. Is. My. TAIL?" hissed Princess Buttons.

"Well. Um. It was in my backpack for a while

and then Nancy nailed it to the wall of our den. But now I'm not really sure, to be honest. Look . . . about the tail. I'm sorry. I honestly thought it was a hot dog."

"SILENCE!" shouted Princess Buttons. The Brain Zapper 3000 was sparking and beeping.

"W-what's that on your head?" asked Ted. "Is it a fun thing or is it a *bad* thing?"

Princess Buttons did an evil cackle.

"This, dear boy, is a Brain Zapper 3000. And I'm afraid it's going to blast you and your sister into smithereens!"

Ted gulped.

"But first I want my tail back," said Princess Buttons, her sharp claws hovering over Ted's face. "Where's that big sister of yours? I know she's around here somewhere!"

"How?" asked Ted.

Princess Buttons whipped out Bin's phone.

"Easy. I tracked her phone. This red dot tells me that she's nearby. Now I want you to scream for your big sis! Scream so that she comes running to me!"

Ted knew what he had to do. But he wanted to ask Princess Buttons one more thing while he still had the chance.

He took a deep breath.

"Listen," he said. "I'm sorry I bit your tail off. But all the other stuff? I just think you've been really mean. All we tried to do was share the food equally among everyone! Don't you think we could forget about this fighting? We could all go back to the Big City, help each other out, share the good times and the bad. What do you think?"

Princess Buttons blinked. And then she laughed.

"I think that you're the stupidest fox I've ever met. I don't like you. I don't like your sister. And I DON'T . . . LIKE . . . SHARING!"

She pointed the Brain Zapper 3000 at Ted.

A voice called down from the top of the Magic Tower.

"HEY. BUTTONS."

Princess Buttons looked up.

"I'VE GOT YOUR TAIL."

And there stood Nancy. She was balanced at the very top of the tower, holding Ingrid's megaphone.

She smirked and waved the scraggly cat tail in the air.

Princess Buttons was so furious she started to shake.

"GIVEMEMYTAILRIGHTNOW!" she screamed.

But Nancy just shrugged.

Princess Buttons went to grab Ted and let out a gasp.

Because Ted had disappeared.

"What the . . . ?" said Princess Buttons.

"Over here!" called Ted, dangling from Frank's talons.

Frank swooped and looped to the top of the Magic Tower and gently plopped Ted down next to Nancy.

Princess Buttons couldn't stand it any longer. She aimed the Brain Zapper 3000 at the foxes and pressed FIRE.

ZZZZZZZAP!

The first laser beam bounced off a corner of the Magic Tower. The force of it threw Princess Buttons onto her back. She struggled back to her feet and took aim again. She pointed the laser beam right at Nancy's head.

ZZZZZZAAAAP!

Nancy threw Princess Buttons's tail into the air at just the right moment. It blew up in an explosion of fur and sparks, and the unpleasant smell of roasted cat wafted through the air.

"MY TAIL!" cried Princess Buttons, dizzy and staggering across the grass. She had one laser beam left.

Using two paws to steady herself, she pointed the Brain Zapper 3000 up at Ted.

Except . . . she couldn't see Ted anymore. Because a gigantic eagle was zooming toward Princess Buttons. It was saying something.

"THE ALIENS!" cried Pamela. "THE ALIENS HAVE LANDED!!!"

Ted, Nancy, and Frank, who were now sitting comfortably in Pamela's chaotic nest, all nodded.

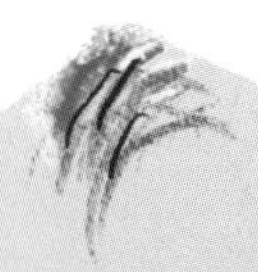

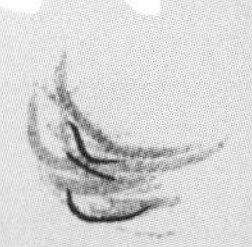

"So they have, Pamela," said Frank. "So they have."

"NO! I'm not an alien!" cried Princess Buttons, seeing Pamela prepare to dive. She unstrapped the Brain Zapper 3000 from her head. "See? I'm just a cat! A normal cat!"

But it was too late.

Ted covered his eyes.

Nancy cheered.

Frank hooted.

And Pamela swooped down from the Magic Tower and bit Princess Buttons's head clean off.

Byeeee!

CHAPTER SIXTEEN
Farewell to Grimwood

After the events of the previous day, Titus and Ingrid had agreed to have another Big Show, seeing as they never quite finished the original one.

"Peppermint?" said Titus, offering a paper bag to Nancy.

"No thanks, Titus." She grinned. "I'm having beef jerky. Don't wanna mix sweet and savory, you know?"

"Thank you, everybody, thank you," said Ingrid from the stage. "Now for our next act, we welcome two talented young ones who've been a marvelous addition to the Grimwood Players this season."

"Ooh, this is them!" said Wiggy, nudging Nancy.

"And I know I speak for many of us," continued Ingrid, "when I say I will be *very* sad to see one of these youngsters go." She clutched a handkerchief to her beak. "But life moves on . . . ceaselessly . . . like waves beating against the shoreline of existence . . ."

Tamara coughed.

"Sorry, yes, anyway, please give a great big Grimwood hooray for TED AND WILLOWWWWWWWW!"

Ted and Willow skipped onto the stage. The lights dimmed.

"Ready?" whispered Willow.

Ted nodded.

The dance began slowly, with Ted and Willow creeping around each other like burglars in an art gallery. Ted appeared to be dressed as a tree, and Willow danced gracefully, pretending to be the wind, the wind, THE WIND, bending Ted's branches.

"Ooh, it's terribly poetic," remarked Wiggy.

But then the music suddenly EXPLODED into frantic joyful disco, and out of nowhere Willow was wearing a multicolored ballgown and Ted was spinning her above his head.

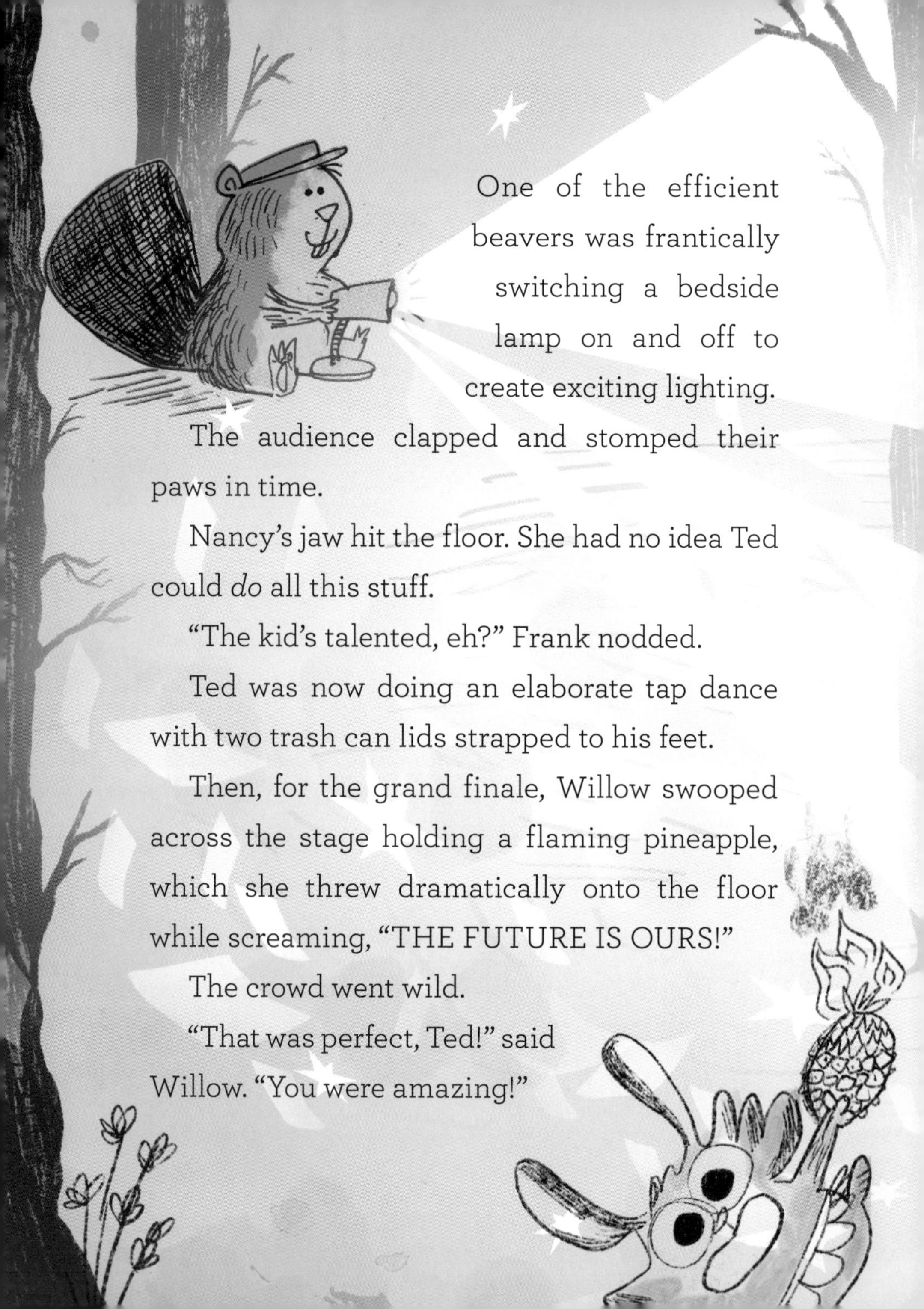

One of the efficient beavers was frantically switching a bedside lamp on and off to create exciting lighting.

The audience clapped and stomped their paws in time.

Nancy's jaw hit the floor. She had no idea Ted could *do* all this stuff.

"The kid's talented, eh?" Frank nodded.

Ted was now doing an elaborate tap dance with two trash can lids strapped to his feet.

Then, for the grand finale, Willow swooped across the stage holding a flaming pineapple, which she threw dramatically onto the floor while screaming, "THE FUTURE IS OURS!"

The crowd went wild.

"That was perfect, Ted!" said Willow. "You were amazing!"

Ted's heart was in his throat. It had been the most intense five minutes of his life, and he had loved every second.

Eventually, the crowd stopped cheering. Ted just stood there, looking out into the crowd. He could see Nancy, Titus, and Frank. The badgers, the rabbits, the squirrels. Even Pamela was perched on the back row, though Frank had insisted on her wearing a muzzle in case she got carried away and ate someone.

"Everyone? C-can I have your attention, please? I just wanted to say something," Ted stammered. A hush fell over the audience. "I just wanna say . . . I've had the most amazing time here in Grimwood. An awful lot has happened. But you guys have all been such good friends to me and Nancy."

"WOOHOO!" cheered Frank and Wiggy.

"Oh, hush," said Nancy, trying to hide a smile.

"I wanted to say thank you," said Ted. "Thank you for being so welcoming and for looking out for us when it mattered the most. As you know, me and Nancy are heading back to the Big City after the show."

There were a few "boos" and Titus honked into Frank's armpit.

"I promise I will never forget you," said Ted. "I will miss you all SO much—especially you, Willow. You're the best friend I've ever had."

Big fat tears rolled down Willow's cheeks.

"But I also need to say thank you to my big sister, Nancy. Firstly, for letting us stay so I could do the show. But also because without her, I wouldn't be here. She's looked after me for as long as I can remember. So even though I'm sad to leave Grimwood, I'm also happy. Because I'll be with her. And wherever she goes, I go. Because she's my home."

WAAAAAH!

Willow and Ted hugged, and he sobbed into his adorable friend's neck. In fact, everyone sobbed into everyone else's neck, because it was the cutest and saddest thing ever, and that was a fact.

While everyone was bawling, Nancy quietly trotted up to the stage.

"Can everyone stop crying?" barked Nancy into the microphone. "Because I've got something to say."

"Ooooooh!" said everyone.

"When we first came here I thought you were all a bunch of weirdos."

"Well, she's not wrong," said Titus.

"And to be honest . . ." continued Nancy, "I *still* think you're a bunch of weirdos. But you've been good to Ted. And you've been good to me, even when I didn't deserve it."

Frank gave her a wink.

"And it's as clear as the snout on my face that I've never seen my little brother look as happy as he has here in Grimwood."

Ted wiped his eyes.

"So I've decided. We're staying."

"Gasp!" gasped everyone.

"That all right with you, Titus?" asked Nancy.

"Oh, but you MUST stay!" boomed Titus. "You fit right in!
BOTH of you."

Ted didn't know what to say.

He hugged Nancy with all of his might while everyone else CHEERED and blew kazoos and someone started playing a jig on a fiddle.

"I love you, sis," he whispered.

"I love you too, bro," whispered Nancy.

She looked around them.

Among the trees she saw the transmission tower, the shopping carts, the stinky pond, Titus's rusty camper, and the bright stars that lit up the inky black sky above them.

“Do you mean it, Nance?” he said. “Can we really stay here?”

“Yeah,” said Nancy. “We can. Grimwood *is* weird. But Grimwood is our home.”